Rescue Dog of the High Pass

by Jim Kjelgaard

Author of "Swamp Cat," etc.

Originally published in 1958.

Jim Kjelgaard has long wanted to tell the story of the gallant dogs who have gone out with the monks of St. Bernard Hospice to rescue travelers lost in the deep snows of the Swiss mountain passes. Unable to find the facts, he decided to reconstruct the tale as he feels it might have been. The result is this very moving story of a simple mountain boy and his devoted dog.

Jim Kjelgaard was born in New York City. Happily enough, he was still in the pre-school age when his father decided to move the family to the Pennsylvania mountains. There young Jim grew up among some of the best hunting and fishing in the United States. He says: "If I had pursued my scholastic duties as diligently as I did deer, trout, grouse, squirrels, etc., I might have had better report cards!"

Jim Kjelgaard has worked at various jobs—trapper, teamster, guide, surveyor, factory worker and laborer. When he was in the late twenties he decided to become a full-time writer. He has succeeded in his wish. He has published several hundred short stories and articles and quite a few books for young people.

His hobbies are hunting, fishing, dogs, and questing for new stories. He tells us: "Story hunts have led me from the Atlantic to the Pacific and from the Arctic Circle to Mexico City. Stories, like gold, are where you find them. You may discover one three thousand miles from home or, as in The Spell of the White Sturgeon, right on your own door step." And he adds: "I am married to a very beautiful girl and have a teen-age daughter. Both of them order me around in a shameful fashion, but I can still boss the dog! We live in Phoenix, Arizona."

Books by Jim Kjelgaard

BIG RED

REBEL SIEGE

FOREST PATROL

BUCKSKIN BRIGADE

CHIP, THE DAM BUILDER

FIRE HUNTER

IRISH RED

KALAK OF THE ICE

A NOSE FOR TROUBLE

SNOW DOG

TRAILING TROUBLE

WILD TREK

THE EXPLORATIONS OF PERE MARQUETTE

THE SPELL OF THE WHITE STURGEON

OUTLAW RED

THE COMING OF THE MORMONS

CRACKER BARREL TROUBLE SHOOTER

THE LOST WAGON

LION HOUND

TRADING JEFF AND HIS DOG

DESERT DOG

HAUNT FOX

THE OKLAHOMA LAND RUN

DOUBLE CHALLENGE

SWAMP CAT

THE WILD HORSE ROUNDUP

RESCUE DOG OF THE HIGH PASS

To

Alice Bedford

CONTENTS

The characters and situations in this book are wholly fictional and imaginative: they do not portray and are not intended to portray any actual persons or parties.

1: THE SCHOOL

Sitting on his assigned portion of the backless wooden
school bench, fourteen-year-old Franz Halle tried earnestly
to concentrate on the Latin text before him. He read,
"Deinde rex perterritus Herculi hunc laborem, graviorem,
imposuit. Augeas—"

Very interesting, he thought, and doubtless very important.
Professor Luttman, who taught the school at Dornblatt, said
so, and Professor Luttman was both wise and educated.
Franz himself had heard the village men say that he could
discuss the classics, politics, history, higher mathematics,
astronomy and the latest method of bloodletting as a cure
for the ague, at endless length and most thoroughly. Franz
tried again.

"Deinde rex—" Surely it meant something or Professor
Luttman never would have assigned it. But what? If only it
were a squirrel track in the snow, a chamois doe trying to
lure an eagle away from its kid, a trout in the cold little
stream that foamed past Dornblatt, or an uncertain patch of
snow that was sure to become an avalanche, it would be
simplicity itself. But written words were never simple, not
even when they were written in the German that Franz
could read.

Franz made one more manful effort. Then he gave up and
devoted himself to looking through the window on the
south side of the school.

The mighty birches that had once grown there, and that had
been so lovely to see when spring clothed their branches in
tightly curled new leaves that looked oddly like baby

lambs, or when the wind set trees and leaves to dancing, had been felled for half a furlong down the mountainside.

Franz smiled wistfully. Furlong—furrow long—the distance a team of oxen could pull a plow without tiring. Now there was a word he understood perfectly. Not that there were any gardens a furlong in length around Dornblatt, for not even the strongest oxen could pull a plow through solid rock. Some of the villagers had even carried dirt, basket by basket, to cover the rocks and form more garden space.

Vaguely it occurred to Franz that there was something he had been doing or should do, but he had forgotten what it was. He continued to look out of the window.

The village spread below him, sturdy log buildings with living quarters for humans on the second floor and stables for the cattle beneath. The villages lined the narrow path that trailed on up the mountain and, eventually, into the mighty Alps. Here and there was a garden patch, for where there was so little land to cultivate, not even one square foot must be wasted. But most of the gardens were beyond the limits of Dornblatt itself. Summer pasturage for the village cattle, and the fields where the villagers cut most of their hay, were far above timber line.

Franz thought again of the birch trees that had been and a twinge of remorse stirred his heart. It was right and just to fell trees, but only when timber was needed for new buildings or wood was required for the village stoves. It was wrong to destroy so many beautiful birches simply because one greedy man had the power to gratify his greed.

The land upon which the school was built had belonged to Emil Gottschalk, the only man in Dornblatt who had managed to acquire any wealth. It was a foregone conclusion that a site for the schoolhouse would be bought from Emil—and this was the only location that he offered. Since practically everybody else in Dornblatt was in Emil's debt, none had dared protest vehemently even though all knew that the schoolhouse, at the very foot of a steep and almost forestless mountain, was directly in the path of an avalanche and, sooner or later, would be destroyed by one.

Emil had prepared for that, too. After selling the site for a school to the citizens of Dornblatt, he had proceeded to sell them the birches. Every man in the village had helped cut and trim the trees, and every horse and ox team had been pressed into service to drag the trimmed trunks to the north side of the school. There the men, including Professor Luttman, had again fallen to and erected a breastwork that probably would stop anything except a major avalanche.

So Dornblatt had its school, but at three times the cost in money and labor that would have been necessary had any of a half dozen other sites that were available—and out of the path of avalanches—been selected.

Franz straightened suddenly and grew tense. A squirrel had emerged from the far side of the clearing where the birches had been and was crossing to the near side. Franz's eyes widened, for this promised both stark drama and excitement. Squirrels lived among the trees, and almost always they were safe as long as they stayed there. But almost invariably they were doomed when they left their arboreal haunts.

Obviously not alarmed, for it was not running fast, the squirrel came a quarter of the way into the clearing. Franz knitted puzzled brows. Latin was a mystery to him, but almost without exception the creatures of the forest were an open book. The squirrel presented a puzzle, for the very fact that it was not running fast proved that it had not been frightened from the forest. It was no baby but an adult, therefore it was acquainted with danger. What had prompted it to risk this foolhardy journey?

As unexpectedly as a sudden wind can whirl a spiral of snow into the air, the squirrel's leisurely pace changed to wild flight. Franz ceased pondering whys and wherefores and lost himself in watching.

From the same side of the clearing where the squirrel had first appeared, a fox emerged from the forest. But rather than choosing a leisurely pace, the fox was running so furiously that it seemed little more than a streak of fur. Franz watched with pounding heart as the animal, whose every leap equalled twenty of the short-legged squirrel's frantic lunges, overtook its quarry.

There was just one possible end, the fox would catch and kill the squirrel before the latter was able to reach the safety of the trees on the other side of the clearing. Then both passed out of Franz's field of vision and, crane his neck as he would, he could no longer see the chase.

He felt a pang of disappointment. He could find no life in a Latin text, but life in its fullest was represented by the fox and squirrel chase.

A split second later, to his vast astonishment, he saw the fox streaking back toward that part of the forest from which it had emerged. Since no squirrel dangled from its jaws, it was evident that the fox had failed to catch its quarry. Then a dog appeared, a half dozen bounds behind the terrified and madly-racing fox. The dog was light tawny in color, with no dark markings. About thirty-two inches high at the shoulder and six feet from tip of its black nose to the end of its tail, it weighed well over a hundred pounds. It was short-haired, square-faced, long-legged, and its tail was curled over its back. Lean of paunch, its shoulders were massive and blocky. Even had it been standing still, instead of running, its great power and strength would have been evident.

Franz smiled. The dog, an Alpine Mastiff, was his own Caesar. Three years ago he'd found it, a whimpering puppy, on the refuse heap where Emil Gottschalk had tossed it to die. Inch by inch, he had nursed it back to health.

He had learned a little of its history, and its roots went very deep. Originating in Asia, probably Tibet, many thousands of years ago, Alpine Mastiffs were brought to Asia Minor by silk merchants. Some fell into the hands of the early Romans, who used them as war dogs. When the Romans crossed the Alps, they took a number of these mastiffs with them. Some became hurt, or a female might give birth to puppies. These were left behind, simply because the marching columns could not afford to be slowed by them. And so, after thousands of years, the Alpine Mastiff found in the Swiss Alps a land very like the Tibet of its forefathers.

Caesar had an almost uncanny ability to adapt himself to the mountains. His huge paws supported him where another dog would have been hopelessly mired. At the height of winter, with Franz on skis and Caesar trailing alongside or behind, the two went where they willed and always safely.

Should the snow be soft, Caesar plowed his own path with his tremendous shoulders and never experienced the least difficulty. Even when all the rest of his body sank out of sight, Franz could always tell where he was by looking at the tip of his tail.

Let the wind blow as it might, and alter the outward appearance of the snow as it would, Caesar still knew the safe trails. He had an inborn foreknowledge of impending avalanches and a feeling for unsafe ice. When the brothers Karsmin were caught in an avalanche and buried beneath seven feet of snow, Caesar found them when all humans failed. Franz was satisfied that the dog had heard their hearts beating.

For all that, Dornblatt had no extra food for dogs. Franz never would have been allowed to keep Caesar had the animal not proven his worth. When the snow lay too deep for any horse or ox to venture forth, it was Caesar who dragged in the firewood. His back could carry as heavy a burden as two strong men were able to bear, so, even though Franz was the only human who could handle him, Caesar earned his way.

Professor Luttman said, "You will please translate the assignment."

Franz, whose body was present but whose spirit had flown to help Caesar chase the fox, paid no attention.

Then he was rudely jerked back into the hall of learning.

"I am talking to you, Franz," Professor Luttman said.

"Me? Oh! Yes, sir," Franz stammered.

"Proceed," Professor Luttman said.

"Well—You see, sir—"

Professor Luttman's kindly, studious face was suddenly very weary. "Did you even hear me?" he asked.

"No, sir," Franz admitted.

"Very well, I'll repeat. Translate the assigned lesson."

"I—I cannot do it, sir."

"Why not?" Professor Luttman asked.

"I do not know it, sir," Franz confessed.

Hertha Bittner, who was always able to do any lesson perfectly, giggled. Her laugh was echoed by the other students. Professor Luttman looked directly at Franz.

"I fear," he said sorrowfully, "that your scholarly instincts and abilities leave much to be desired. For two years I have tried earnestly to teach you, and I question whether you have yet mastered the simplest portion of any subject at all. It is my considered opinion that your time will be far more constructively spent if you devote it to helping your father. Will you be so good as to go home and tell him what I have said?"

"Yes, sir."

Franz left the schoolroom, his cheeks burning. Caesar's meeting him at the door lifted none of his shame and embarrassment, but did provide solace. Laying his hand on the big mastiff's neck, Franz struck directly away from the school.

At least, he could take the long way home.

2: SHAME

Franz left by the north door. He began to run at once, with Caesar keeping effortless pace beside him.

With its base only a few rods from the schoolhouse, the mountain on the north side rose so steeply that the youngsters of Dornblatt used it as a practice site for their first lessons in mountain climbing. There were numerous sheer bluffs, and such soil as existed was thickly sprinkled with boulders that varied from the size of a man's head to the size of a Dornblatt house.

Shame was the spur that made Franz run, for as he sped between the school and the great log and earth barrier that the men of Dornblatt hoped would keep a major avalanche from crushing the school, it seemed to him that every pupil and Professor Luttman must be looking at him and jeering. He imagined the superior smile on Hertha Bittner's pretty lips, the scornful curve of Willi Resnick's mouth, the sardonic contempt that would be reflected in Hermann

Gottschalk's cold eyes, and in his mind he heard Professor Luttman say, "There goes Franz Halle, the failure! There goes one too stupid to understand the true value of learning! Look upon him, so that you may never be like him!"

Franz's cheeks flamed and his ears were on fire. He might have chosen not to attend the school and everyone would have understood. But of his own free will he had become a student, and by Professor Luttman's order he was ignominiously expelled. Nobody in Dornblatt could ever live such a thing down.

Then Franz and Caesar were across the clearing and back in the hardwood forest.

Franz slowed to a walk, for the great trees that grew all about had always been his friends and they did not forsake him now. They formed a shield that no scornful eyes could penetrate, and as long as he was in the forest, he would know peace. His own practiced eye found a big sycamore that was half-rotted through, and he marked it for future firewood. The sycamore was sure to fall anyway, and in falling it would certainly crush some of the trees around it. But it could be felled in such a fashion that it would hurt nothing, and a healthy young tree would grow in its place.

Franz stole a moment to wonder at himself. Other Dornblatt boys and girls, some of whom were much younger than he, had no trouble learning Professor Luttman's assigned lessons. Why should that which was written in books be so hopelessly beyond his grasp while that which was written in the forest and mountains was always so easy to read?

He spied a squirrel's nest, a cluster of leaves high in a birch tree, and beneath the same tree he found a crushed and rounded set that meant a hare had crouched there. A jay tilted saucily on a limb and peered at Franz and Caesar without scolding. Jays never shrieked at him, Franz thought, as they did at almost everyone else, and he was sure that was because they knew he was their friend.

The two friends wandered on, and when they reached a little open space among the trees, Franz halted to tilt his head and turn his eyes heavenward. High above him towered a rock-ribbed peak, so tall that even in summer its upper reaches were snowbound. Franz stood a moment, contented just to look and grow happier in the looking.

Unknown to his father, or to anyone else in Dornblatt, he had climbed that peak. Little Sister it was called, to distinguish it from an adjoining peak known as Big Sister. Carrying only his ropes and alpenstock, he was accompanied by the mastiff until blocked by a wall that the dog could not climb and up which Franz could not rope him. He had ordered Caesar to wait and gone on alone. From the topmost eminence of Little Sister, he had viewed a breath-taking array of other peaks.

But there was infinitely more than just a view.

Franz had never told even Father Paul, Dornblatt's kindly little parish priest, how, as he stood on the summit of Little Sister, he had felt very close to Heaven—he, simple Franz Halle who could not even get ahead in school. He had never told anyone and he had no intention of telling.

Now, as he looked up at Little Sister, remembering that wonderful feeling, Franz became almost wholly at peace.

The school seemed very far away, part of a different world. This, and this alone, was real. It seemed to Franz that he always heard music, with never a jarring or discordant note, whenever he was in the forest or climbing the mountains.

Presently he reached another downsloping gulley and halted on its near rim to look across. On the far rim was a farm that differed from the houses in Dornblatt because quarters for the people, a neat chalet, were separate from the building that housed the stock. It was the home of the Widow Geiser and had been the best farm anywhere around Dornblatt.

Then, three years ago, Jean Geiser had gone into the mountains to hunt chamois. He had never returned, and ever since the Widow Geiser had been hard put to make ends meet. Her two sons, aged four and six, were little help and no woman should even try doing all the work that a place such as this demanded. The Widow Geiser still tried, but it was rumored that she was heavily in debt to Emil Gottschalk.

Caesar pricked his ears up and looked at the goat shed. Following the dog's gaze, Franz saw a brown and white goat, one of the widow's small flock, come from the rear door, squeeze beneath the enclosing pole fence and make its way into a hay meadow. It stalked more like a wild animal than a domestic creature and its obvious destination was the forest. Should it get there, it would be almost impossible to capture the animal again.

Franz turned to his dog. "Take her back, Caesar."

Silent as a drifting cloud, for all his size, Caesar left Franz and set a course that would intercept the fleeing goat. He came in front of the escaping animal. The goat halted and stamped a threatening hoof.

Franz almost saw Caesar grin. The mighty dog could break this silly animal's spine with one chop of his jaws, if he wished to do so, but he was no killer. He advanced on the goat, that tried and failed to break around him. Then he began edging it back toward the paddock. When the goat squeezed under the dog leaped over and continued to herd the escapee toward the pen.

Laughing, Franz ran forward and arrived at the goat pen just in time to meet the Widow Geiser, who came from her chalet.

Despite the man's work she had been doing, the Widow Geiser was still attractive enough to furnish a lively subject for discussion among Dornblatt's unattached bachelors. If the fact that she was also proprietress of a good farm detracted nothing from her charms, that was natural enough.

Now she asked, "What's the matter, Franz?"

"Caesar and I were walking in the forest when we saw one of your goats trying to escape. I ordered Caesar to drive it back."

"Thank you, Franz. Hereafter I must keep that one tethered. She has tried to run away so many times. Won't you come in for some bread and milk?"

"I thank you, but the hour grows late and I must turn homeward."

"The sun is lowering," the Widow Geiser agreed. "Thank you again, Franz, and come again."

"I shall look forward to it."

With Caesar padding beside him, Franz started down the gulley toward Dornblatt and as he did so, his uneasiness mounted. He had delayed meeting his father for as long as possible, and now he admitted to himself that he feared to face him. But the meeting could no longer be postponed.

Franz made his way through Dornblatt to his father's house. Caesar, who preferred to remain outside, regardless of the weather, curled up in front of the cattle shed. Franz tried to be resolute as he climbed the stairs to the living quarters, but, once at the door, he halted uncertainly.

Then, taking his courage in both hands, he entered the single room that served the Halles as living-dining-bedroom. The ceiling and wall boards were scrubbed until they shone; the floor was of red tile. There was a big fireplace with a wooden chimney and a great, gleaming-white porcelain stove bound by brass rings. Spotless pots and pans hung from wooden pegs. A table and seven straight-backed wooden chairs occupied the center of the room. At the far end, where lowered curtains might separate them, were the beds where slept Franz's father and mother, his four young sisters and himself.

Franz's mother sat silently in the chimney corner, and the fact that she was not doing something with her hands was all that was necessary to prove that much was amiss. His four overawed sisters hovered at the far end, near the beds.

Franz Halle the elder met his son. Six-feet-two, storm and wind and the mountains that hemmed him in had written their own tales on his wrinkled face. By the same token, the very vigor of the life he'd led had left him straight as a sapling and endowed him with iron muscles. His clear blue eyes, gentle for the most part, now glinted like the sun slanting from glacier ice.

He said, "Professor Luttman came to see me!"

"Yes, sir," Franz answered meekly.

His father demanded, "Have you nothing else to say?"

"I'm sorry," Franz answered in a low voice.

"Once I hoped you would be a farmer," the elder Halle said, "so I set you to plowing. I found the plow abandoned and the oxen standing in their yokes while you chased butterflies. Then I thought you would be a herdsman, but I found the cattle lowing to be milked while you roamed the forest with your dog. I apprenticed you to a cobbler, and you attached the heels where the soles should have been. I asked a lacemaker to teach you his trade, and in one day you ruined enough material to do away with a week's profit. I decided you must surely be a scholar, and now this!"

Franz said humbly, "I think I am not meant to be a scholar."

"Is there anything you are meant to be? The one task you do, and do well, is chop wood with your ax."

Franz brightened a little. "I like to chop wood."

"May a chopper of wood be a future family man of Dornblatt, where everyone chops his own?" his father demanded. "Think, Franz!"

"Yes, sir," Franz said.

There was a knock at the door and the elder Halle opened it to admit Father Paul. For all his lack of stature, the little priest somehow took instant command.

"I have come to help," he said, "for I, too, have heard."

"It is past your help," the elder Halle told him sadly. "My only son seems destined to become a nobody."

Father Paul smiled. "Despair not, my friend. You'll feel better in the morning. I think the boy has not yet been guided into the way he should go and I have a suggestion. At the very summit of St. Bernard Pass there is a hospice. It was erected by the revered Bernard de Menthon, many centuries past, and its sole purpose is to succor distressed travelers who must cross the Alps. I think I may very well find a place there for Franz."

"As a novice of the Augustinian Order?" the elder Halle asked doubtfully.

"Not quite." Father Paul smiled again, at Franz this time. "Novices must clutter their minds with Latin and any number of similar subjects. He may be a lay worker, or maronnier. Would you like that, Franz?"

"Oh, yes!" Franz's soaring imagination sped him out of Dornblatt to the fabled Hospice of St. Bernard.

"Will he go now?" the elder Halle asked.

"Hardly," Father Paul replied, "for it takes time to arrange such matters. He may very well go next summer. Meanwhile, I know you will find some useful occupation for him."

Franz's father said, "He can cut wood."

3: THE GREEDY VILLAGER

Franz sank his razor-sharp ax in the raw stump of a new-cut birch and used both hands to close his jacket against an icy wind that whistled down from the heights. He looked up at the cloud-stabbing peak of Little Sister and smiled. Yesterday, the snow line had been exactly even with a pile of tumbled boulders that, according to some of the more imaginative residents of Dornblatt, resembled an old man with a pipe in his mouth. Today, it was a full fifty yards farther down the mountain.

Caesar, who never cared how cold it was, sat on his haunches and, disdaining even to curl his tail around his paws, faced the wind without blinking. Franz ruffled the big dog's ears with an affectionate hand and Caesar beamed his delight. Franz spoke to him.

"Winter soon, Caesar, and it is by far the very finest time of all the year. Let the children and old people enjoy their spring and summer. Winter in the Alps is for the strong who can face it, and for them it is wonderful indeed."

Caesar offered a canine grin, wagged his tail and flattened his ears, as though he understood every word, and Franz was by no means certain that he did not. The dog understood almost everything else.

Franz wrenched his ax from the birch stump, and, dangling it from one hand so that the blade pointed away from his foot, he went on. As his father had said, nobody in Dornblatt could hope to live by cutting wood and that alone. Every household must have a supply, for wood was the only fuel, but since every able-bodied householder cut his own, it naturally followed that they cared to buy none.

Franz was still unable to remember when he had enjoyed himself more completely. Other men of Dornblatt regarded the annual wood cutting as an irksome chore, and life in the forest the loneliest existence imaginable. As long as he could be in the forest, it never occurred to Franz that he was alone.

There was always Caesar, the finest of companions. There were the mice, the hares, the foxes, the various birds, and only yesterday Franz had seen thirty-one chamois on their way from the heights, that would soon be blanketed beneath thirty to forty feet of snow, to seek winter pasturage in the lowlands. There had been two magnificent bucks, plus a half a dozen smaller ones, but Franz had not mentioned the herd because there were a number of eager chamois hunters in Dornblatt. Should they learn of the chamois and succeed in overtaking them, they might well slaughter the entire herd. Chamois, Franz thought, were better alive than dead—and it was not as though there was a lack of food in Dornblatt. It had been a good year.

As he walked on, Franz pondered his expulsion from Professor Luttman's school. The sting was gone, much of the shame had faded, and there were no regrets whatever. Franz knew now that he simply did not belong in school, for his was not the world of books. If, on occasion, he met a former classmate, and the other asked him how he was getting on, he merely smiled and said well enough.

Franz remained more than a little troubled about Professor Luttman, though. He was a good and kind man who seldom had any thoughts that did not concern helping his pupils. Franz felt that somehow he had failed Professor Luttman.

The heavy ax hung almost lightly from his hand, as though somehow it was a part of his arm. Franz had always regarded his ax as a beautiful and wonderful tool. He could strike any tree exactly where he wished, fell it exactly where he wanted it to fall and leave a smoother stump than Erich Erlich, who owned the finest saw in Dornblatt.

Always choosing one that was rotten, deformed, or that had been partially uprooted by some fierce wind and was sure to topple anyhow, Franz had spent his time felling trees. Then he had trimmed their branches. With a great bundle of faggots on his own back and a greater one on Caesar's, he had hauled them to his father's house. Finally, he had cut the trunks into suitable lengths, and such portions as he was unable to carry, he and Caesar had dragged in.

His father had finally ordered him to stop. Wood was piled about the Halle house in every place where it was usually stored and many where it was not. There was enough to last the family through this winter and most of next. If any more were brought in, the Halles would have to move out.

Franz had continued to cut wood for those who were either unable to gather their own or who, at the best, would find wood cutting difficult. There was Grandpa Eissman, once a noted mountaineer, who had conquered many peaks but lost his battle with time. Old and stooped, able to walk only with the aid of his cane, Grandpa Eissman's house would be cold indeed this winter if he and he alone must gather wood to heat it. Then there was Jean Greb, who'd lost his right hand in an accident on Little Sister. There was also—

Franz knew a rising worry as he made his way toward a tree he had marked for cutting. There were not so many unable to gather their own wood that he could keep busy throughout the winter, and what then? Wood cutting was the only duty with which his father would trust him.

He thought suddenly and wistfully of the Hospice of St. Bernard. More than eight thousand feet up in the mountains, the Hospice must have been snowbound long since. There were few days throughout the entire year when snow did not fall there and, when it was deep enough, the monks and maronniers—Father Paul's strange term for lay workers—must get about on skis. Franz felt confident of his ability to keep up with them, for he had learned to ski almost as soon as he'd learned to walk. Surely the Hospice must be one of the world's finest places, but Franz seemed no nearer to going there than he had been last summer.

Father Paul had talked with him about it once more, and Franz had broached a very troublesome problem. If he were accepted as a maronnier, might Caesar go with him?

He would see, Father Paul promised, and he had gone to see. He returned with no positive answer and Franz dared not press the issue. Surely the great Prior of St. Bernard Hospice had problems far more important than whether to accept so insignificant a person as Franz Halle as a lay worker.

Franz reached the tree he had already selected, felled it with clean strokes of his ax and trimmed the branches. Cutting them into suitable lengths, he shouldered a bundle, tied another bundle on Caesar's strong back and took them to Jean Greb's house. Jean greeted him pleasantly. He was a youngish man with wavy blond hair and clear blue eyes.

"It is very kind of you to provide me with wood, Franz, when I find it so very difficult to provide my own."

"It is my privilege," Franz said. "If I did not go out to cut wood, I would have to languish in idleness."

Jean, who appeared to have some troublesome thought on his mind, seemed not to have heard.

"Will you come in and have some bread and cheese?" he invited.

Franz smiled. "Gladly. Wood cutting works up an appetite."

Franz dropped his own burden of wood, then relieved Caesar of his load. The big mastiff settled himself to wait until his master saw fit to rejoin him. Franz greeted Jean's pretty young wife and his three tousle-topped children and seated himself opposite Jean at the family table. Jean's wife placed bread, milk and cheese before them.

Franz waited for his host to begin the meal and became puzzled when Jean merely stared at the far wall. Something was indeed troubling him. Presently he explained.

"I once thought Dornblatt the finest place on earth!" he exclaimed bitterly. "But there is a serpent among us!"

The puzzled Franz said, "I do not understand you."

"Emil Gottschalk!" Jean burst out. "The Widow Geiser is heavily indebted to him and now he says that, if she does not pay the debt in full, and within ten days, he will take her farm and all else that is hers!"

"He cannot do such a thing!" the astounded Franz cried.

"Aye, but he can," Jean said. "Which is more, he will and there is nothing any of us may do except offer asylum to the widow and her sons!"

A short time later, Franz walked gloomily homeward, his thoughts filled with the pleasant little farm and the attractive young woman who was fighting so valiantly to keep her home. If there was anything anyone could do, somebody would have done it. Professor Luttman was a very clever man. He would not let Emil Gottschalk take the Widow Geiser's farm if there was a way to forestall him.

A week later, the snow came to Dornblatt. It whirled down so thickly that it was impossible to see more than a few yards in any direction, and it left fluffy drifts behind it. Eighteen hours later, there was another snow and the people of Dornblatt took to their skis.

The snowfall was followed by two days of fair weather, then the first great storm of the winter came. It was so fierce that even the men of Dornblatt would not venture forth until it subsided.

Franz was at the evening meal with his family when he heard Caesar's challenging roar. Footsteps sounded on the stairs. A moment later Hermann Gottschalk, Emil's son and Franz's former classmate, stumbled into the room.

"Father!" he gasped. "He is lost in the storm!"

4: NIGHT MISSION

Hermann Gottschalk stood a moment, took a faltering step and almost fell. With a mighty effort, he stayed erect and spread his feet wide, the better to brace himself.

Franz's father leaped from his chair, hurried to the youth, passed a steadying arm around his shoulders and escorted him to the chair he had just vacated. White-faced and trembling, Hermann sat limply down and leaned forward to grasp the edge of the table. Franz's father nodded toward his mother.

"Some wine please, Lispeth."

Franz's mother was already at the wine cask. She drew a cup, brought it to the table, and the elder Halle held the cup to Hermann Gottschalk's lips. Hermann sipped, gasped mightily, took another sip, and the warming wine did its work. He relaxed his hold on the table and sank back in the chair.

"Tell us what happened," the elder Halle said gently.

Hermann's voice was a husky whisper. "Father and I had to see the Widow Geiser. It was a fine morning and we expected no trouble as we started out on our skis. The storm was upon us suddenly, and within minutes it was so fierce that we could no longer see where we were going. It was some time before we knew we must have gone beyond the Widow Geiser's and—"

Franz's father let him rest a moment and then, "Go on," he urged.

"We turned back to Dornblatt, but again we were unable to see where we were going or guide ourselves by landmarks. Father became very tired. He fell, then fell again. Finally, he cried, 'I can go no farther! Save yourself!' I tried to carry him and could not. I knew I must get help."

"What time did you leave your father?" the elder Halle asked.

"I cannot be certain, but think it might have been an hour before night fell," Hermann answered. "I went on, though I could not be sure at any time that I was coming to Dornblatt. Then I heard a dog bark and guided myself by the sound."

Franz's father asked, "How long ago was that?"

"Again I cannot be sure, but I was no great distance from Dornblatt. Immediately after hearing the dog, I broke a ski. Since that made the remaining ski useless, I threw both away and plowed through the snow. It took me much longer to reach the village than it would have had the ski not broken."

Franz pondered the information. Emil and Hermann Gottschalk could have gone to the Widow Geiser's only to evict her, and trust Emil to wait until after all crops were harvested and stored! But that was in the past. For the present, a man was lost in the storm.

Franz thought over the affair from every angle. It was probable that Hermann and his father had gone a considerable distance past the Widow Geiser's before they realized they were lost and turned back. On the return trip, they had set a reasonably accurate course. Hermann had left his father an estimated hour before nightfall. Soon after darkness descended, or approximately within the past forty-five minutes, a barking dog had guided him to Dornblatt.

However, probably, since leaving his father his rate of travel had been that of an exhausted youngster. He had also broken a ski, which, by his own admission, was responsible for more delay. Emil Gottschalk, Franz decided, was approximately forty-five-minutes' skiing time from Dornblatt and the proper direction in which to seek him was toward the Widow Geiser's.

But there were so many other possibilities that entered the picture. Just how far beyond the Widow Geiser's were Hermann and his father when they turned back? Or were they beyond her place at all? In such a storm, with both lost and neither able to see, it would be comparatively easy to travel up the slope, and, without ever reaching the Widow Geiser's farm, both Hermann and his father might be sincerely convinced that they were far past it. Or had they gone down the slope? Or—

The elder Halle turned to his son. "You know what we must do?"

"I know," answered Franz.

"What route do you intend to follow?" his father asked.

"I'll work toward the Widow Geiser's with Caesar," Franz told him. "I'll try to retrace the path I think Hermann might have followed. If we do not find Mr. Gottschalk, I'll cast back and forth with Caesar and depend on his nose."

"A good plan," his father said, "and, since you are the only one who has a dog that might be depended upon to find a lost man, it will be best for you to work as you see fit. I'll rouse the villagers and we'll search the same area, with each man assigned to his own route. Take my pistol, for when Emil is found, one shot will announce to all that the search is ended and at the same time bring help. I will carry my rifle and signal with it."

"Loan me some skis!" Hermann pleaded. "I would search, too!"

"No," Franz's father said. "You are near exhaustion and, should you venture out before you've rested, there will be two lost in the storm. Stay here and rest in Franz's bed."

Franz stole a glance at his former classmate, who had always seemed such an awful snob but toward whom he could now feel only sympathy. Faced with a grave problem, Hermann had been courageous enough, and, despite the fact that some villagers would be sure to consider the entire incident a judgment of God because Emil Gottschalk would have impoverished the Widow Geiser, Franz knew that it was only a judgment of the storm.

In Dornblatt, few winters ran their course without someone getting lost—and not all were found. Franz was glad that his father had said, in Hermann's hearing, "when Emil is found," and not, "if he is found."

Franz put on his ski boots and his heavy coat with the hood, and thrust his father's immense, brass-bound, bell-mouthed pistol into his belt. Franz Halle the elder dressed in a similar fashion, slung the rifle over his shoulder, and the pair left the house together.

Comfortable in their stable beneath the house, the cattle stamped their hoofs, munched their fodder and never cared how much snow fell. Caesar sprang from his snow tunnel, shook himself, and came forward to push his nose into Franz's mittened hand.

The two Halles took their skis from beneath the overhanging ledge, where they were stored when not in use, and harnessed them to ski boots. A ski pole in either hand, the elder Halle paused a moment before setting out to rouse the able-bodied men and boys from Dornblatt's snow-shrouded houses.

He said, "We will come as quickly as possible," and was gone.

Franz waited another moment. Within fifteen minutes, or twenty at the most, all Dornblatt would know of the lost man and all who were able would be in the search. But there was something else here, something more sensed than seen or felt.

His father had declared that he, Franz, was fit only for cutting wood. But it was quite evident now that the elder Halle also thought his son a capable man in the mountains. If he did not, he would never let him go off alone on a night such as this.

A pride that he had seldom felt—or seldom had reason to feel—swelled within Franz. He was no scholar and he was a complete dolt at most skills and crafts. But it was no small thing to be considered an accomplished mountaineer.

Caesar, who might easily have broken trail, was too sensible to do so when he might follow the trail already broken by Franz's skis. He stayed just far enough behind to avoid stepping on the tail of either ski.

Franz let him remain there for now. Emil Gottschalk would surely be farther from Dornblatt than this. When the time came, and Caesar was ordered to go ahead, he'd do it.

A minute afterwards, the falling snow hid the village as completely as though it had never been and Franz and Caesar were alone in the night. The boy remained undisturbed. He had never feared the mountains or the forest and he was not afraid now.

He started southward, traveling downslope, for the wind screamed from the north and Hermann Gottschalk had been guided into Dornblatt by a dog's bark. Even Caesar's thunderous bark would be heard at no great distance against such a wind. But any sound would carry a long way with it. Hermann must have come in from the south.

Just how far south had he been when he heard the dog bark? Hermann himself did not know. But when he turned toward the barking dog, in addition to plowing through deep snow, he had been fighting an uphill slope and a powerful wind. Without skis, his progress must have been painfully slow. Therefore, he could have been no great distance from the village.

Franz curled the hood of his jacket around his face to keep flying snow out of his eyes. It made little difference as far as visibility was concerned, for, in the stormy night, he could see less than the length of a ski pole anyhow.

Except for those who were too old or disabled, everybody in Dornblatt must use skis or remain housebound from the time the deep snows fell until they melted. Most were past masters of ski travel, but Franz had an extra touch, an inborn feeling for snow, that set him apart. He was not afraid of becoming lost or of breaking a ski, as Hermann Gottschalk had, probably when he blundered into a tree trunk.

When Franz thought he had gone far enough south, he turned west, toward the Widow Geiser's. Again he used his mountain lore and knowledge of snow to analyze what might have happened.

Leaving his father, Hermann probably had tried to set a straight course. Undoubtedly the powerful wind had made that impossible. While Hermann thought he was traveling due east, he had also gone slightly south. Franz set a course that would take him slightly north of west.

Now he must consider Emil Gottschalk. Even though he was lost in the storm, Emil, a lifelong resident of Dornblatt, was not one to surrender easily, and he would know what to do. Even though he was unable to stand, he would crawl to the lee of a boulder or copse of trees and let the snow cover him. His own warm breath would melt a hole and assure a supply of air. Even though such a bed was not the most comfortable one might imagine, any man buried beneath snow would never freeze to death.

Franz made a mental map of all the boulders or copses of trees on the course he was taking that Emil might seek. When he thought he was reasonably near the place where Emil lay, he began to zigzag uphill or down, depending on which was necessary to reach each of the shelters he had already marked in his own mind.

Whenever he came to such a place, he watched Caesar closely. But at no time did the dog indicate that there was anything worth his interest. Franz passed the farthest point where he had calculated he might find Emil Gottschalk.

In all this time, he did not see any of the other searchers, but that was not surprising. The area to be covered was a vast one. Also, someone might have passed fairly close in the snow-filled darkness and would not have seen or heard him.

He began to worry, but kept on for another half hour, for Emil might be farther away than he had thought possible. Finally, sure that he had passed the lost man, Franz climbed higher up the mountain and turned back toward Dornblatt.

Now he set a course south of east, trying as he did so to determine exactly how far the wind might have veered Hermann from a true course. His anxiety mounted when he found nothing.

At what Franz estimated was two hours past midnight, the snow stopped falling and the stars shone. Now there was light, and, even though it was only star-glow, it seemed dazzling when compared with the intense darkness that had been. Franz set a new course, back toward the Widow Geiser's.

He was descending into a gulley when Caesar stopped trailing and plunged ahead. Plowing his own path with powerful shoulders, he went up the gulley to a wind-felled tree that cast a dark shadow.

On the tree's near side, Caesar began to scrape in the snow. Franz knelt to help, removing his mittens and digging with bare hands. He felt cloth, then a ski boot.

Franz rose and fired the pistol that would bring help from the men of Dornblatt. Then he resumed a kneeling position and continued to help Caesar dig Emil Gottschalk from his snowy couch.

5: THE "MARONNIER"

No herald robin or budding crocus announced that spring was coming to Dornblatt. Rather, at first for a few minutes just before and just after high noon and then for increasingly longer periods each day, snow that had sat on the roof tops all winter long melted and set a miniature rain to pattering from the eaves. The snow blanket sagged, the ski trails collapsed, and every down-sloping ditch and gulley foamed with snow water.

The chamois climbed from their hidden valleys to their true home among the peaks, birds returned, cattle departed for lofty summer pastures, farmers toiled from dawn to dark— and Father Paul came to visit the Halles.

He arrived while the family was at the evening meal, for during this very busy season there was almost no other time when all members of a family might be together. Franz's father rose to welcome him.

"Father Paul! Do accept my chair and join us!"

"No, thank you." Father Paul waved a hand and smiled. "I have already supped and this fine chair of the Alps shall serve me very well."

Father Paul chose a block of wood from the pile beside the stove, upended it, and seated himself. The elder Halle took back his chair and resumed his interrupted meal.

"I have just returned from Martigny, where I visited Emil Gottschalk," Father Paul said. "He is greatly improved, and he seems reconciled to the loss of one of his feet."

"To lose a foot is a bad thing," the elder Halle said seriously.

"But it might have been much worse," Father Paul pointed out. "Were it not for Franz and Caesar, Emil would have lost his life, too."

"I did nothing," Franz murmured.

He stared hard at his plate, remembering. Both of Emil's feet were frozen, and there'd been nothing for it except to take him to the hospital at Martigny. He'd been there ever since, and, while Franz was glad that he would live rather than die, any credit for saving him belonged properly to Caesar. Franz had his own vexing problem.

Finding Emil Gottschalk had made him a person of no small importance in Dornblatt. But why be important when not even his own father would trust him with any task except cutting wood, and everybody in Dornblatt had long since had all the wood they could use? Even skiing in the forest while Caesar followed behind or plowed ahead had not occupied all of Franz's time, and the days had become tedious indeed.

The once-bright dream of becoming a maronnier, or lay worker, at the Hospice of St. Bernard had faded with the passing of time. If the Prior intended to consider him at all, surely he'd have done so before this—and in his own heart Franz did not blame the Prior. Why should the Prior of St. Bernard want anyone whose sole talents consisted of wood cutting and mountain climbing, when his own village did not even want him?

"So you did nothing?" Father Paul asked. "The remark does you compliment, for modesty in the very young is far more becoming than in the old." He began to tease. "I must say that you are wholly correct. Had you stayed home that night, rather than venture forth with Caesar, Emil would have been rescued anyhow. I haven't the least doubt that Caesar would have done it all by himself."

Franz murmured, "I'm sure he would."

"Oh, Franz, Franz," Father Paul sighed. "Would that I could teach you!"

"I've tried everything I know," the elder Halle said, a bit gruffly. "There simply is nothing more."

"You are too harsh," Father Paul chided him.

"I must be harsh," Franz's father said. "The boy will shortly be a man. Can he take his proper place among the householders of Dornblatt if he knows nothing except how to cut wood, run the forests and climb mountains? Do not condemn me, Father Paul. If I did not love the boy, would I care what happens to him? But I repeat, I can think of nothing more."

Father Paul said, "I can."

Franz's father and mother turned quickly toward him. His four sisters leaned eagerly forward in their chairs and even Franz was interested. An unreadable smile played on Father Paul's lips.

"Tell us," Franz's father pleaded.

"Very well," Father Paul agreed. "Had there been no news of Emil, I'd have had reason to come here, anyway. When I returned from Martigny, there was a message waiting—"

He stopped for a moment, and Franz's father begged, "Father Paul, please go on!"

Father Paul smiled. "It was a message from the Prior of St. Bernard Hospice. Franz has been chosen as a maronnier, and he is to report as soon as possible."

"No!" Franz whooped.

His father looked sternly at him. "Please, Franz! Speak quietly or do not speak!"

"Let the boy shout," Father Paul reproved him. "There have been so many doors to which he could not find the key. At long last, one has swung wide and beckons him in."

Franz's puzzled father said, "I do not understand you."

Father Paul explained. "I mean that, from this time on, Franz may go forward."

"Caesar, too?" Franz asked breathlessly.

"Caesar, too," answered Father Paul. "I promised I'd inquire about your dog, and I kept my promise. You should know, however, that Caesar will be expected to pay his way with his work."

Franz exclaimed happily, "Caesar and I like work!"

"Had I thought otherwise, I never would have recommended you," said Father Paul. He looked at Franz's father and mother. "Well?"

"It's so far," Franz's mother said worriedly, "and so strange."

"It is neither as far nor as strange as you think," Father Paul reassured her. "It is true that the summer is much shorter, the winters much colder and the snow much deeper than you ever know them to be in Dornblatt. But, like everyone else who serves at the Hospice, Franz has been reared in the mountains. I assure you that he will fit in very well."

"He may go," the elder Halle said.

"He—may go," Franz's mother quavered. "How—how shall we prepare him for the journey?"

"Supply him with enough food and clothing for the walk," Father Paul replied. "Since snow may fall in St. Bernard Pass any day of the year, I suggest that he have at least one heavy coat. After he arrives, the Hospice will provide for him."

Franz's mother said brokenly, "Thank you, Father Paul."

6: FATHER BENJAMIN

Swinging the pack on his shoulders with an ease born of long practice, Franz turned to look down the slope he had just climbed. Bearing a similar pack, Caesar turned with him.

Only the memory of his mother's tears when they exchanged their farewells kept Franz from shouting with joy. This was far and away the most fascinating experience of his life.

The route, as explained by Father Paul, had proven absurdly simple. Franz must go to Bourg and follow the Valley of the River Drance. After that, he couldn't possibly get lost, for the only path he'd find must take him over St. Bernard Pass. But the way had proven anything except routine or monotonous to Franz.

Leaving the hardwoods, the forest with which he was most familiar, he had entered, and was still in, a belt of evergreens. He laughed happily.

Jean Greb, who by no means lacked imagination, had once told Franz that to see one tree was to see all trees. But that great spruce only a few yards down the path, whose wide-spreading branches allowed room for nothing else, was very like—Franz stifled the thought that the greedy spruce might be compared to greedy Emil Gottschalk, for it ill-befitted anyone to think badly of a human being who was already in enough trouble. But the spindly larch whose summer needles were just beginning to grow back was remarkably like Grandpa Eissman, with his straggling hair and stubble of beard. The fat scotch pine, that seemed to hold its middle and laugh when the wind shook it, might well be fat and jolly Aunt Maria Reissner. The knobs on the trunk of a young pine reminded Franz strongly of knobby-kneed young Hertha Bittner.

Franz turned to go on, thinking that Jean Greb was wrong and that all trees were not alike. They differed as greatly as people. Probably every person in the world had his or her counterpart in some tree.

A bustling stream snarled across the path, hurried down the slope and, as though either bent on its own destruction or in a desperate hurry to keep its rendezvous with the sea, hurled itself over a two-hundred-foot cliff. Foam churned up in the pool where it fell and the sun, shining through it, created a miniature but perfect rainbow.

Franz stopped for a long while to watch, for in such things he found deep pleasure. Then he and Caesar leaped the stream and went on.

It was noticeably colder than it had been at the lower altitudes and Franz recalled Grandpa Eissman's explanation for Alpine temperatures. Pointing to a ledge a bit less than three thousand feet up the side of Little Sister, he had said that, when warm summer reigned in Dornblatt, autumn held sway there. Since sixty degrees was regarded as summer in Dornblatt, and thirty-two degrees, the freezing point, might reasonably be considered autumn, it followed that the temperature dropped approximately one degree for each three hundred feet of altitude.

But Franz did not feel the cold. This was partly because, sometimes in steep pitches and sometimes in gentle rises, the path he followed went steadily upward. Excited anticipation added its own warmth, so that presently he removed his coat and tied it to the pack.

In the late afternoon, they emerged from the evergreen forest into the Alpine region. This was where the cattle found rich summer pasturage, and where thrifty Swiss farmers cut much of their hay. Here were stunted pines, juniper, dwarf willows and millions of narcissuses and crocuses in full bloom. High on the side of a rocky crag, Franz spied a sprig of edelweiss and was tempted to climb up and pluck it. But the day was wasting fast and the climb up the crag might be more difficult than it appeared. Spending the night on the face of the crag would mean a cold camp indeed. It would be wiser to go on to the rest hut.

The sun was still an hour high when he reached it, a rock and log hut a little ways from the path. Franz opened the door, dropped his pack and removed Caesar's. Then, with the mastiff padding beside him, he started into the meadow, carrying the small hatchet that was a parting gift from his father.

There was wood already in the hut. But it was not only possible but probable that some wayfarer too exhausted to cut his own wood might reach the shelter, and to find fuel at hand would surely save a life. Able-bodied travelers were obligated to gather their own.

But so many wayfarers had come this way, and so many seekers of fuel had gone out from the hut, that Franz had to travel a long distance before finding a tree, a small pine whose withered foliage proved that it was dead, so suitable for firewood.

Bracing his back against a boulder, the boy pushed the tree over with his foot rather than cut it, for the dried trunk broke easily. He chopped out the remaining splinters with his hatchet and, dragging the tree behind him, started back toward the hut.

He was still a considerable distance from it when Caesar, who had been pacing beside him, pricked up his ears and trotted forward. The dog looked fixedly in the direction of the structure. Coming near, Franz saw that he was to have a companion.

The newcomer was a tall, blond young man, wearing the garb of an Augustinian monk. Since he was in the act of divesting himself of the pouch wherein he carried food and other necessities of the road, evidently he had just arrived. He looked up, saw Franz and Caesar, and his white teeth flashed as he smiled.

"Hello, fellow travelers!" he called cheerfully. "I am Father Benjamin."

More than a little overawed because he was to share the hut with such distinguished company, Franz said, "I am Franz Halle and this is my dog, Caesar. We are pleased to have you with us."

Father Benjamin laughed. "I am sure the pleasure shall be mine. Hereafter, I may truthfully say that I shared a hut with Caesar. If you'll wait a moment, Franz, I will bring my portion of the wood."

Franz said, "This is enough for two."

"So I am to be your guest?" Father Benjamin asked. "I am indeed honored." He looked keenly at the boy. "Aren't you a bit young to travel this path with only a dog as companion?"

"I must travel it," Franz told him. "I go to the Hospice of St. Bernard, where I am to become a maronnier."

"A maronnier, eh?" Father Benjamin asked. "And what inspired you to become such?"

"I am too stupid to be anything else," Franz answered.

Father Benjamin's laughter rang out, free as summer thunder and warm as a June rain. Puzzled, Franz could only stare. After a bit, the monk stopped laughing.

"I do crave your pardon!" he said. "But it is rare to receive such an honest answer to a well-intended question. Nor do I think you are stupid, young Franz Halle. Those who are never say so. Surely you are clever in some ways?"

"I can cut wood, climb mountains, get about on snow and work with Caesar," said Franz.

Father Benjamin said gravely, "Then you are surely coming to the right place."

Franz began taking bread, cheese and cakes from his pack. "What does maronnier mean?" he asked.

"Moor," replied Father Benjamin. "The Moors are a warlike people from a far country. They robbed and stole, and one of the finest places to do so, since many travelers must go through it, was the Pass of St. Bernard. When our sainted Bernard first came this way, he was merely Bernard de Menthon, a youth not yet in his twenties. He and those with him found the Pass held by a group of Moorish bandits, whose chief was named Marsil. Bernard, most devout even then, held his crucifix erect and put the entire band to flight."

"With a crucifix alone?" Franz asked incredulously.

"It is thought by some that the clubs and axes carried by Bernard and his party and wielded with telling effect on Moorish skulls, helped out," Father Benjamin admitted, "but we like to believe that his faith and courage are what counted most. Bernard went on into Italy, where in due time he became Archbishop of Aosta. Travelers through the Pass continued to tell of Moorish bandits, so Bernard returned to rout them."

"And did he?" Franz asked breathlessly.

"He did indeed," answered Father Benjamin. "But other tales were also coming out of the Pass. They were stories of travelers who died in the terrible storms that rage across these heights in winter, and there were a great many such unhappy tales. Bernard determined to build a hospice, a shelter for all who needed it, at the very summit of the Pass. The Moors, led by the same Marsil whom Bernard had previously defeated, knew they could never prevail against such might. So rather than fight him again, they chose to become Christians and join Bernard. Since they could not be priests, they became lay brothers, or maronniers."

"It is a wonderful story!" Franz gasped.

Father Benjamin said seriously, "One of the most wonderful ever told. This Pass has been in use since mankind began to travel. The Roman legions used it to invade Gaul. Hannibal took his army through it to invade Italy. Countless others have traveled through it, and countless people still do and will. We who are charged with its keeping consider it the finest privilege of all to serve at the Hospice of St. Bernard."

"What is it like?" Franz asked.

"It is cold, my young friend," replied Father Benjamin. "There are winter days of fifty below zero. Snow in the Pass lies forty-five feet deep. The wind blows constantly and fiercely and shifts the snow about so that the entire landscape may change from one day to the next. Sometimes there is a complete change in an hour, or even minutes. Some might think it the most miserable life imaginable, but we who serve at the Hospice know it is the finest!"

"How long will you be there?" Franz asked.

Father Benjamin told him, "Even though only men born to the mountains and skilled in mountain arts are chosen for service at the Hospice, and even though our spirits may be strong, the bodies of the strongest cannot endure the trials we must face for more than twelve years. But during those years, and quite apart from ministering to souls, all of us save lives. That is our reward."

Franz asked, "Do you save everyone?"

"Unfortunately, no," said Father Benjamin. "Many are still lost. But in the more than seven centuries that have passed since Bernard de Menthon erected the Hospice, an army of people who otherwise would have been victims of the snow have lived to return to their loved ones and carry on constructive work."

"Do travelers use the Pass all winter?" Franz continued his eager questioning.

"Indeed they do," Father Benjamin assured him. "The path is open to the next rest house, where we shall sleep tomorrow night, and travelers may safely make their own way that far. From there on to the Hospice, some five miles, is the real danger area. There is another rest house five miles down the south slope. When possible, which is when the weather is not so bad as to make it impossible, one of us visits each rest house every day. Such wayfarers as may be there are then guided to the Hospice and, of course, on down to the next rest house."

Franz asked, "What is your greatest difficulty?"

"Choosing a safe trail," Father Benjamin declared. "I've spoken of the fierce winds and shifting snows. Each time we go down to a rest house, we face an entirely different landscape, where a misstep might well mean death to us and those we guide. But come now, Franz, is it not time to stop talking and start supping?"

"Indeed it is," Franz agreed, "and my mother prepared a great store of food. I shall be honored if you will share it."

"And I shall be honored to share," said Father Benjamin.

7: THE HOSPICE

The wind that screamed between the high peaks which kept
a grim vigil over both sides of St. Bernard Pass proclaimed
itself monarch.

Man was the trespasser here, the wind said, and let who
trespassed look to himself. The only kindness he could
expect was a quick and painless death. This was the haunt
of the elements.

Overawed and more than a little afraid, Franz tried to speak
to Father Benjamin, who was leading the way. The wind
snatched the words from his teeth, whirled them off on its
own wings and hurled mocking echoes back into the boy's
ears. Franz dropped a hand to the massive head of Caesar,
who was pacing beside him, and found some comfort there.

Franz thought back over the way they had come.

The inn at Cantine, where he had passed the night with
Father Benjamin, was not a half hour's travel time behind
them, yet it was an entire world away. The inn was still
civilization. This was a lost territory. The Alpine meadows
had given way to rocks and boulders, among which grew
only moss and lichens. The wind was right and no man
belonged here.

Franz shuddered. They had skirted chasms where a fall
meant death. They had passed beneath rising cliffs
whereupon lay boulders so delicately balanced that it was
almost as though an incautious breath would set them to
rolling, and an avalanche with them. In the shadier places
there had been deep snow, and at no point was the

permanent snow line more than a few hundred yards above them.

With a mighty effort, Franz banished his fears and regained his self-control. This was the Grand St. Bernard Pass, one of the easiest of all ways to cross the Alps. The altitude was only about eight thousand feet. When Franz stood on the summit of Little Sister he had been almost a mile higher. The old, the crippled and children used this Pass regularly.

Franz told himself that he had been overwhelmed by the reputation of the Pass, rather than by any real danger. It went without saying that so many perished here simply because so many came here. The boy fastened his thoughts on practical matters.

Supplies for the Hospice, Father Benjamin had told him, were brought to Cantine on mules and carried from there by monks and maronniers. It was not that mules were unable to reach the Hospice—sometimes they did—but, at best, it was a highly uncertain undertaking. From about the middle of June until the autumn storms began, the Pass was considered safe enough so that rescue work might be halted during that period, but an unexpected blizzard might come any time. Thus, though in due course the muleteer probably would be able to get his animals back down, as long as they were marooned at the Hospice they'd be consuming valuable and hard-to-gather hay.

Father Benjamin turned and spoke, and Franz heard clearly. "We have a fine day for our journey."

Franz tried to answer, could not, and Father Benjamin smiled and waved him ahead. The boy grinned sheepishly. He should have remembered that it is almost impossible to speak against such a wind but relatively easy to speak, and be heard, with it. He edged past Father Benjamin and said, "Indeed we have."

He was suddenly calm and no longer afraid. This was no foreign land and it was not a place of devils. It was his homeland. It was St. Bernard Pass, where, of his own free will, he had wanted to become a maronnier. He belonged here.

Father Benjamin put his mouth very close to Franz's ear and shouted, "Do you still think you have chosen well?"

Franz answered sincerely, "Very well."

"Good!"

Father Benjamin indicated that he wanted to pass and Franz let him do so. The monk turned to the icecapped peaks on the right of the Pass.

"There are Rheinquellhorn, Zappothorn, Fil Rosso and Pizzo Rotondo," he said, then turned to the left. "There we see Pizzo della Lumbreda, Pizzo Tambo and Pizzo dei Piani. They will become your firm friends."

Franz shouted, "They are already my friends."

When Father Benjamin frowned questioningly, Franz smiled to show that he understood and the pair went on. The wind suddenly sang a song instead of snarling threats. Lowlanders who understood nothing except a warm sun might flinch from such weather. But, as Father Benjamin had said, it was indeed a fine day—if one happened to be a mountaineer.

Presently Father Benjamin stopped again. "The Hospice," he said.

Franz looked, more than a little astonished. He hadn't had the faintest notion of what he might expect, but certainly it was not the massive, fortresslike structure that, though still a long ways off, seemed as prominent as any of the peaks. Presently the boy understood.

The Hospice must be visible from as great a distance as possible. Many an exhausted traveler, coming this far and sure he could go no farther, would find the strength to do so if he could see a refuge.

Father Benjamin pointed out the principal buildings. "The chapel," he said. "The refectory, where meals are eaten and guests entertained, the sleeping quarters, the house of the dead—"

Franz looked questioningly at him and Father Benjamin explained. "The mortal remains of many who die in the snows are never claimed. At first they were interred beneath the Hospice floor. Now, in the event that someone will claim them some time, they go into the house of the dead. Some have been there for a hundred years."

Franz felt a proper awe. A hundred years was a long time to be dead. But to be dead a hundred years in a place such as this, which was shunned by even the cliff and cold-loving edelweiss, must indeed be dreadful! Franz consoled himself with the thought that the dead have no feeling. No doubt those who rested in warm valleys and those who waited in this grim house would both awaken when Gabriel blew his trumpet.

They drew nearer, and Franz saw a little lake from which the ice had not yet melted. That was fitting and proper and altogether in keeping. Some of these Alpine lakes were ice-free for fewer than thirty days out of the whole year.

Then they came to a stable beneath one of the buildings and Franz met his immediate superior.

He was big as a mountain and bald as a hammer. His eyes were blue as glacier ice that has been swept clean by the broom of the wind, and at first glance they seemed even colder. His face, for all his size, was strangely massive. Perhaps because of his very lack of other hair, his curling mustaches seemed far longer than their eight inches. For all the cold, he wore only a sleeveless leather jacket on his upper body. It hung open, leaving his midriff, chest and biceps bare. Rippling muscles furnished more than a hint of great strength.

Franz thought at first glance that he was a dedicated man, one who is absolutely devoted to his work, for he treated Father Benjamin with vast respect.

"Anton," Father Benjamin said, "I want you to meet the new maronnier, Franz Halle. Franz, this is Anton Martek. He will instruct you in your duties here."

"Is good to have you." Anton Martek extended a hand the size of a small ham. "Your dog work? Yah?"

"Oh, yes!" Franz said eagerly. "See for yourself that he carries a pack even now!"

Caesar wagged up to Anton Martek, who ruffled the dog's ears but continued to look at Franz.

"Packing is not all of work." He scowled. "Is he a spit dog, too?"

"A what?" Franz wrinkled puzzled brows.

With a sweeping circle of his right arm, Anton offered a near-perfect imitation of a dog walking around and around while the meat on a spit roasted. Franz warmed to this huge man. Anton's ice was all on the outside. Inwardly, he was gentle as the fawn of a chamois.

"Not yet," Franz said. "But I know we can teach him."

"Yah," said Anton. "We teach him."

Father Benjamin laughed. "You two seem to be getting along very well together, so I'll leave you alone."

Anton said respectfully, "As you will, Father," and turned to Franz. "Come."

Franz followed him into the stable, that was windowless, except for rectangles of wood hung on wooden hinges that now swung open to admit the sunlight. The place had a familiar smell the boy was unable to define until he remembered that the same odor dominated his mother's kitchen, and that it was the odor of complete cleanliness.

"Where are the cattle?" he asked.

Anton replied, "Down in the pasture."

"Down?"

"Yah. You villagers bring them up. We take them down. There is no pasture here."

He led Franz to a great pile of hay at one end of the stable and gestured. "You sleep here."

Franz laid his pack down and relieved Caesar of his, not at all displeased. There are, as he knew from experience, sleeping places not nearly as comfortable as a pile of hay.

"We get you some more covers soon," Anton promised. "But for now there is work. You will clean the stable."

"But—" Franz looked in bewilderment at the already spotless stable. "It is clean!"

"Ha!" Anton snorted. He stalked to a rafter, ran one huge finger along it, discovered a tiny speck of dust and showed it to Franz. "See? You will clean the stable."

Franz said meekly, "Yes, Anton."

8: A FREE DAY

It had not been easy to coax Caesar inside, even into a stable, but Franz had succeeded both in getting him in and in persuading the big Alpine Mastiff to sleep at his feet. Now, as the wind screamed through St. Bernard Pass and the frost cut like a sharp knife, Franz grinned to himself.

He understood that the three other maronniers at the Hospice; the novices, or apprentice priests; the Aumonier, who welcomed guests and dispensed charity; the Clavandier, who watched over all stores; the Sacristan, whose duty it was to take charge of the Chapel; the Abbe, who watched over the novices; the four Canons, whose authority was exceeded only by that of the Prior, and even the great Prior himself, slept in unheated cells.

He was not positive about this because anyone as lowly as he could never be sure about the doings of people as mighty as they. For all he knew, the Hospice would collapse if he spoke to any of the Canons, and the mountains themselves would tumble if he even looked at the Prior. But he thought it was true.

If it was, then he, Franz Halle, the humblest of the humble maronniers, had by far the finest sleeping quarters in Great St. Bernard Pass. With fragrant hay as a mattress, plenty of blankets, a dog to keep his feet warm, and the four gentle cows of the Hospice to add their warmth to the stable, let the wind scream as it would and the frost crackle as it might. He would never care.

Caesar shifted his position at Franz's feet, to bring his head nearer the boy's right hand. Franz took his hand from beneath the blankets to tickle Caesar's ears, and a worried frown creased his forehead.

Besides Caesar, he had two firm friends at the Hospice, Father Benjamin and Anton Martek. The other two maronniers were surly individuals who kept much to themselves. Franz did not even know their names. The novices, boys about Franz's own age, were much too busy with their own duties to have any time for a mere maronnier. Naturally it was unthinkable, aside from attending devotions, to intrude on the world of the priests. Father Benjamin, who came to the stable at regular intervals, had made a real effort to strengthen a friendship that began when he and Franz came up the path together.

Anton Martek worried Franz, and the dawn to dark work Anton demanded had no bearing on it, for the boy did not mind working long hours. But there was Caesar, too. The mastiff had worked willingly beside his master while they freighted hay or wood from the lower reaches or carried supplies from the inn at Cantine. But winter was fast approaching, and when it came, there would be almost no packing for Caesar, and everything that lived at the Hospice must necessarily earn its own way.

Since there was little else, Anton and Franz had tried their valiant best to make a spit dog of Caesar. But the great animal, who did so many things so well, seemed wholly unable to adjust to what he doubtless considered the low comedy of turning a spit. On the first trial, he whirled in his tracks and snatched at and ate the roast he was supposed to be turning. When Anton fashioned a harness that made it impossible for him to turn, Caesar's nearness to the fire, with its unaccustomed warmth, made him so uncomfortable that he simply lay down and refused to move at all.

A longer pole that put him farther away from the fire offended his dignity. Rather than pace slowly, so that the meat would turn slowly and roast evenly on all sides, he whirled at such speed that it was a marvel the roast stayed on the spit. Weights on his paws, designed to slow him down, aroused his stubbornness. Rather than turn the spit at all, he pulled it completely apart and let the roast fall into the fire.

Shouting threats accomplished nothing. Caesar knew his own strength and, providing it was consistent with his dignity, he would work because he loved Franz. He would not be bullied. Rewards in the shape of meat dangled enticingly before him were haughtily rejected. Caesar would not be bribed, either.

The stubborn Anton had not abandoned hope and was still determined to make a spit dog of Caesar, but, in the darkness, Franz's worried frown deepened. The mastiff was equally determined that he would not turn the spit, therefore, not even Anton could make him do it.

An anguished little moan escaped Franz. If Caesar were declared useless and banished from the mountain, life in St. Bernard Pass, that had become so very fine, would be so very bleak. A second time Franz reached out to ruffle the big mastiff's ears.

"Try!" he whispered fiercely. "Try hard, Caesar!"

The dog licked his hand. Thus comforted, his body cushioned by soft hay, warmed by blankets and Caesar, and with the cattle adding their warmth to the stable, Franz never heard the wind scream and never thought of the frost.

He was awakened by Anton Martek, who lighted his way
into the stable with a glass-shielded candle. Caesar rose
and wagged his tail to greet this new friend whom he had
come to like so well, and Franz sat sleepily up in bed.
Anton hung his candle-lantern on a wooden peg.

"It is time to be up," he scoffed good-naturedly. "The day is
for working."

"It is not day yet," Franz protested.

Anton said, "Soon it will be."

Anton, who was entirely willing to let Franz clean the
stable as long as he kept it spotless, but who never
permitted anyone except himself to handle the cows or their
products, began to groom his charges. He always followed
the same procedure. After the cows were clean as comb and
brush could make them, he would wash their udders with
warm water. Then he would milk, care for the milk and
clean the cows all over again.

Franz impulsively asked a question that had long tickled
his curiosity, but that he had never dared ask before. "Why
do you stay here, Anton?"

The huge man turned toward him, comb in one hand and
brush in the other, and for a moment his eyes were so
terrible that Franz shrank before them. The eyes softened
the merest trifle.

"Why do you ask that?" Anton asked quietly.

"I—I've just wondered, and I—I'm sorry if I offended you,"
Franz stammered.

Anton said, "You meant well and I will tell you. At one time, I lived in Martigny, where I was famous for my strength. There was another man who was neither bad nor good. He was much like the jay that always chatters but seldom says anything worth the listening, and he was given to spasms of rage. I saw him strike a child, a little boy, who should not have been taunting him but was. I told the man that he must never again strike a child. The man struck at me and—"

Anton's voice trailed off into a husky whisper. He stared for a moment at the far wall of the stable, then continued, "I struck back and—I killed him. I never meant to kill, and I knew I did not, for it is a terrible thing to take the life of a fellow human. But the only others who knew I never intended to kill were the Fathers at the Hospice. They gave me refuge. They cared for my body as well as my spirit. They restored my faith in God and in man. They made a man from what had been a beast. That is why I am happy to serve them and why I shall never leave this place!"

"I understand!" Franz exclaimed. "And I don't believe you ever intended to kill either!"

"Thank you, little Franz." Anton's rare smile flashed. "Now, if you will get your breakfast, I will care for my babies here."

Caesar at his heels, Franz left the stable and made his way to the kitchen. Caesar sat down outside the door. Paul Maurat, the surly maronnier who presided over the kitchen, kept his domain as spotless as Anton insisted the stable be kept. Certainly, he would never dream of letting a dog invade his kingdom.

A tall, string-thin and apparently ageless man, he motioned Franz to a chair, served him barley gruel, black bread, cheese, and milk and apparently forgot all about him. Franz finished his meal and went outside, where he was rejoined by Caesar, and the pair returned to the stable.

"Back so soon?" Anton asked. "Would Paul not feed you?"

"He fed me very well," Franz declared, "but I have been thinking."

"And what has occupied your thoughts?" Anton asked.

"A very great man I knew in Dornblatt," Franz answered. "His name is Professor Luttman, and he is a teacher, and it is in no way his fault because I am too stupid to grasp what he tried to teach."

"Not everyone may understand the wisdom that is written in books," Anton said.

"That I know," agreed Franz. "But I cannot escape a feeling that I betrayed Professor Luttman. I am sure he knows I am just a maronnier at St. Bernard Hospice. Father Paul, the village priest who acted on my behalf in order that I might come here, would have told him. I am also sure that, on the day he expelled me from his school, he knew I would always hold a humble station."

"He is a wise man?" Anton questioned.

"Very wise," Franz replied.

"The wise do not have to be told that the world is made up of the humble and the mighty," Anton said. "They know that much from their own wisdom. Think no more about it."

"I cannot help thinking about it," Franz said in a troubled voice. "I would like to prove to Professor Luttman that a maronnier's is a good life. Since I cannot, are you ready to have me start cleaning the stable?"

"Today I clean the stable," Anton said. "It is not that you have failed to do it very well, but you have worked hard and long. This shall be a free day for you and Caesar."

"Oh, Anton!"

"Go along now." Anton's smile was pleased.

Caesar at his heels, Franz again left the stable. He braced himself against the wind as soon as he was outside and paused to consider. It was fine to have a free day, but in St. Bernard Pass, exactly what did one do with it? The surrounding peaks invited him. But though the only evidence of foul weather to be lay in an overcast sky, Franz had an uneasy premonition that something besides an ordinary storm was in prospect. It would never do to be caught on a mountainside while such a storm raged.

Just then Father Benjamin came around a corner of the refectory. "Hello, young Franz!"

"Father Benjamin!" Franz cried happily, then added, "Anton has given me the day to spend as I wish."

"How very fine!" said Father Benjamin. "I am on my way to the inn at Cantine. It isn't really necessary, since there seems to be little likelihood of snow, but any travelers who await there may feel easier if they have a guide. Do you want to come along?"

Father Benjamin, Franz and Caesar made their way down the rocky path and found four people waiting to cross the mountain. They were an elderly man, his middle-aged daughter, a boy about Franz's age and a girl not yet in her teens.

Father Benjamin spoke reassuringly to them. "There is nothing to fear. We will guide you to the Hospice, and after you have rested there, you will be guided to the rest house on the opposite slope."

As they all started up the slope, Franz's uneasiness grew. The wind sang a song of trouble. He comforted himself with the thought that Father Benjamin was better able than he to judge what might happen.

They were halfway between the inn and the Hospice when a sudden, blinding blizzard swept down upon them.

9: THE BLIZZARD

The girl and the boy drew a little nearer to Father Benjamin. Their faith showed in their eyes, as though nothing ill could befall them while they were under the guardianship of a priest from the Hospice. The Augustinian, their actions said, might even halt the blizzard by raising his hand and commanding it to stop.

But the elderly man, who had spent his life in the mountains and knew the real danger of such storms, cried out in fear. His fright communicated itself to the woman ... and spread from her to the boy and girl, who would not have been afraid at all had they not seen for themselves that their elders were frightened.

Father Benjamin took instant, firm command.

"Have you never before seen snow fall?" he thundered. "Be quiet and act sensibly!"

"Yes, Holy Father," the elderly man said humbly.

Father Benjamin turned to Franz. "I will guide. You bring up the rear with Caesar."

Franz fought to keep his voice from trembling as he replied, "Yes, Father Benjamin."

He let the others pass and fell in behind. He knew that Father Benjamin wanted him there to keep the little group from straying or straggling, and he was proud to be trusted with such responsibility. At the same time, he was more than a little afraid.

The winter snows in Dornblatt had been fierce enough; often it was impossible to see the house next to that in which one lived. But the snows of Dornblatt had remained within the scope of human understanding, and humans had always been able to cope with the worst of them.

This was a wild beast uncaged, a snarling, raging thing that had burst the bonds of control the instant it began. With the blizzard only minutes old, already they were walking in snow that came halfway to the tops of their shoes. Though each person stayed as close as possible to the one in front of him, Franz could barely make out the form of Father Benjamin, who was leading the way.

He had a sudden, terrifying thought that they were just mites, specks of dust in an inferno of snow. The mad wind would whirl them away as it whirled the snowflakes. When the wind finally lulled and dropped them somewhere in the immensity of the Alps, they would still be as nothing, for a human being is small indeed compared with a mountain.

Resolutely Franz put such fears behind him. Man's body, and that alone, had never conquered the Alps or anything else. Man's spirit was the true conqueror, and spirit would see them safely through this blizzard. The thought gave back to him his old serenity and calmness.

The girl, walking in front of him, slipped and almost went down. Franz caught her elbow and helped her regain her balance.

"Careful, little sister!" he shouted, to make himself heard above the wind. "The snow is a cold bed!"

She turned and gave him a grateful smile, and Franz knew that his recovered confidence had imparted itself to her. They hurried to catch up with the others, who had gained a few feet. Franz looked questioningly at Father Benjamin.

Fortunately, the wind was blowing up the mountain, so that they did not have to fight it. But cross currents and gusty little side eddies blew the snow in every imaginable direction. There was no landmark whatever; even the peaks were hidden. Franz, who had been this way many times, knew that he himself hadn't the faintest notion as to whether or not they were on the path. Did Father Benjamin know?

Again he put the thought behind him. Regardless of anything else, Father Benjamin must act as though he knew. Just as he had exploded the travelers' fears with the thunder of his words when the blizzard began, so he must now inspire them with confidence by showing confidence himself. To do otherwise meant panic, and panic meant that all were lost.

Father Benjamin plowed through a knee-deep drift and halted. The others grouped around him.

"We will have a short rest." Even though the Augustinian had to shout, he seemed as serene and unruffled as though he were addressing some of his fellow priests at the Hospice. "This is the first snow and we may very well get along without skis. But it is foolish to exhaust ourselves."

"Salvezza!" the old man moaned. "Salvation! Or shall we find any?"

The woman said, but with no great conviction, "This good Father will lead us safely to the Hospice."

"He cannot!" asserted the old man.

The young girl said, half-contemptuously, "You have no faith."

Father Benjamin spoke kindly to the frightened old man. "Be of good cheer, Grandfather, for in a short time we will be at the Hospice. After you have rested, go to the Chapel and give thanks to our good Saint Bernard, who founded the Hospice so that travelers such as you might live."

"I, too, shall give thanks to Saint Bernard," the girl declared confidently.

"And I," the boy echoed.

Father Benjamin turned again to the frightened old man. "Can you fear when mere children cannot? Let us go."

With Caesar beside him, Franz took his place at the rear. He turned his head constantly from side to side, hoping for a break in the draperies of snow that hid all save that which was immediately before him. If there were such a rift, even for a second, he might see a familiar boulder, cluster of boulders, or mountain peak that would tell him they were on the path.

He had a growing fear that they were not, for who could find a path in a storm such as this? The landscape changed beneath his very eyes. A drift that had been was suddenly no longer when the wind blew it into snow dust. A drift that had not been was present when the snow-laden wind wearied of its burden and dropped it.

Franz placed a hand on Caesar's head and found in the massive dog the comfort he never failed to discover there. He and Caesar had faced many storms together, though none had been as terrible as this. But, as Father Benjamin had said, it was just a snowstorm.

Suddenly, Caesar left Franz's side, bounded ahead, hurled himself on Father Benjamin, seized the priest's habit in his great jaws, and pulled him over backwards.

For a moment, Franz stood petrified, too astonished to even move. The four travelers stared, unable at once to understand what had happened or what they were staring at.

Franz recovered his wits and ran forward. He knelt beside Father Benjamin and Caesar, who maintained a firm grip on the priest's robe, and shouted, "I'm sorry, Father Benjamin! I do not know why Caesar would do such a terrible thing!"

"Make him let me go!" Father Benjamin's voice was stern and indignant.

"Let go, Caesar!" Franz commanded. "Let go, I say!"

Caesar closed his eyes, took a firmer grip and dragged Father Benjamin six inches backwards through the snow. The angry priest turned to grapple with him.

There was a soft hissing, as though a thousand snowflakes had fallen on a hot stove all at the same time. A bridge of snow, upon which Father Benjamin would have walked had he taken one more forward step, fell in and revealed the yawning chasm across which it had formed.

Caesar released his grip on Father Benjamin's habit, sat down beside the priest, and licked his hand with an apologetic tongue.

"He knew!" Father Benjamin gasped. "That is why he pulled me back!"

Franz said, "Caesar always knows the safe trails."

"Then you should have told us so, little Franz," Father Benjamin said.

"I had not wanted to trespass upon your authority," the boy explained.

Father Benjamin said, "When lives are at stake, it is never a question of authority but one of common sense. Can Caesar guide us safely from here?"

Franz answered unhesitatingly, "Yes."

"Then let him lead."

Franz said, "Go, Caesar."

The great mastiff struck off at a thirty-degree angle to the course they had been following. He broke a drift with his massive shoulders.

"I am done," the old man wailed piteously. "Leave me and go on."

Father Benjamin said, "We will rest."

"I am truly spent!" the old man cried. "I cannot walk another step."

Franz staggered through a drift already broken by Caesar and groped with his hands. They found a brick wall.

It was the Hospice.

10: THE HOUSE OF THE DEAD

Franz braced the sole of his shoe against the blade of his shovel, took a big bite of snow and threw it high above his head. Even cows, Anton Martek had told him—or especially cows—might lose their faith if they could never see daylight.

How could they see daylight if the windows of their stable were darkened by snow? And how could the snow be removed unless someone shoveled it away? Franz thought grimly that, at last, he knew why the handles of the shovels at St. Bernard Hospice were a full three feet longer than any in Dornblatt.

Caesar, lying on the snow six feet above the boy's head, wagged an amiable tail and grinned a canine grin. Franz glared at him.

"You might well smile!" he glowered. "You do no work at all! You refuse even to turn the spit!"

Caesar's tail wagged harder and his jaws parted a bit more. A little worm of worry gnawed at Franz's heart. Since the deep snows had started, except to go down to the rest house with Father Benjamin whenever it was the latter's turn to go, the mastiff had been idle.

Anton had worked patiently and endlessly to make him turn the spit—and he was still working at it. But Caesar had discovered a simple ruse that foiled the most cunning scheme Anton could devise; he merely lay down, wagged his tail, beamed agreeably and refused to move at all. Not even Anton cared to drag a hundred-and-fifty-pound dog around and turn the spit with him.

Franz looked beseechingly up at the big mastiff, who was still lying on the snow and interestedly observing his master.

"You should learn to do it!" he begged. "Father Benjamin already knows that you will not work! Soon Father Martin or Father Stephen will discover that Anton and I have been taking turns revolving the spit for you. They will inform one of the Canons, who is sure to tell the Prior. Then you will be sent away from the Hospice, which is entirely right and good and as it should be. The Fathers are not men of wealth, who can afford to maintain such a big, lazy loafer as yourself in idleness!"

Caesar wagged his tail a little harder, as though he were being complimented. Franz looked sternly at him, but could not find it in his heart to scold any more.

"It will be very right and very just if you are sent away," he said sadly, "but it will leave me so very lonesome. Caesar, you must try!"

Franz turned back to his shoveling, fastening his heart and mind on the one ray of hope that remained to him. Since the day of the blizzard, when Caesar had brought them safely to the Hospice, Father Benjamin had emphatically declared that any dog able to do such a thing was priceless. But he was not going to be readily accepted.

There had been dogs at the Hospice since its founding; tradition said that Bernard de Menthon himself had had one. But tradition said also that it was the work of the priests and maronniers at the Hospice to succor travelers. That was why only men born to the mountains and skilled in mountain arts could be accepted for service there.

It had been that way for seven hundred years, said Father Benjamin, and anything that has existed for seven centuries is not lightly discarded. Franz should be of good cheer, and while so being, though he needn't dishonestly conceal the fact that Caesar was doing no work, he needn't advertise it either. Gentle persuasion, according to Father Benjamin, was far more effective than raging or bullying when it came to breaking a wall of custom that was seven hundred years old.

Meanwhile, whenever it was Father Benjamin's turn to go down to either rest house, he would take Caesar with him. Sooner or later, he would prove the dog's value.

Franz sighed and dug his shovel blade into the last of the snow. Caesar had accompanied Father Benjamin on every trip. But on every trip Father Benjamin made, the weather had been so fine that there had been no need for a rescue or any other kind of work. Franz threw the last of the snow out of the hole, climbed out himself and at once slipped his feet into the skis that awaited him.

The snow at this altitude was hard and granular and not at all similar to the soft stuff that often covered the lower reaches. The hard snow, plus Caesar's huge paws, kept him from sinking more than a few inches, and he rose to greet his master with furiously-wagging tail. Franz caught up his shovel, smoothed the snow he had thrown out and turned to look about him.

The Grand St. Bernard Pass was indeed locked in the grip of winter, with snow piled high about the Hospice and drifts lying at intervals. But the day had started out very well, and Fathers Stephen and Martin had gone down to the rest houses on the north and south slopes, in order to bring up any travelers waiting there.

Franz turned uneasily on his skis. The day was still fine, but there were a few clouds where none had been earlier and an undercurrent that spoke of fury to be. It was a hint that only a born mountaineer could feel at all—but Franz resolutely banished his fears. Father Stephen had had three years of experience at the Hospice and Father Martin seven. They were well able to take care of themselves.

Franz moved to the stable door, slipped out of his skis and entered. Anton Martek, sitting on a pile of hay and honing an ax, looked up and grinned.

"Tomorrow," he prophesied, "you shall have all of it to do over again."

"So you sense the storm coming, too?" Franz asked.

"I sense nothing," Anton said serenely, "for to do so is very silly. I live for the moment that is, not the one that will be, and that proves me either a great fool or a very wise man. I do not know which and do not care, but anyone knows that snow may fall at any time now in Grand St. Bernard Pass. Therefore, it is evident that you will do your shoveling all over again tomorrow."

Franz said, "It is very great labor."

"It is life at the Hospice," returned Anton. He patted Caesar's massive head. "If you did not like the life, you would not be here. As for this great loafer, it is no wonder he enjoys it, for he has nothing whatever to do."

"If the Prior finds out," Franz said worriedly, "Caesar will not be living at the Hospice any more."

"Trust in God and Father Benjamin," Anton advised. "By the time the Prior discovers the supposed worthlessness of this mighty eater, Caesar's worth will be known."

"It should be known by this time," Franz pointed out. "Father Benjamin told of how Caesar prevented his falling into the crevasse and then found a safe path. Some of the Fathers smiled at him, for they said it was no great blizzard, anyhow."

"As it was not," Anton remarked.

Franz went on, "Some said it was God Who saved us."

"And do you doubt that it was?" Anton asked.

"No," Franz admitted, "but Caesar had something to do with it, too. Why cannot he be given due credit?"

"You have not learned the lesson of patience," Anton told him. "That is not surprising, because no youth has. I tell you everything will be all right."

"I hope so," Franz said gloomily. "Now, since all this thinking has pained me, I will clean the stable."

"A worthy endeavor," Anton said, "and one well calculated to remove your mind from your own troubles."

Caesar threw himself down on a pile of hay, pillowed his head on his paws and went to sleep. Franz started cleaning the stable. He sighed again. It would be nice if he were wise, like Father Benjamin or even like Anton, for then he would know so many things that otherwise he could never hope to know.

Since he was stupid and knew nothing except how to work with his hands, he must find contentment in such work. Presently he found it and became so absorbed in what he was doing that he was startled by Anton's voice, saying, "We must close the shutters, for it is starting to snow."

Franz looked up to discover that the stable, never bright as long as snow was heaped around the shutter openings, had grown noticeably dimmer. He hurried to help close the shutters. Anton lighted his candle lantern and hung it on the peg. With the shutters closed, the scream of the wind died to a soft moaning.

Caesar rose to pace beside Franz, as though in so doing he was somehow standing between his master and the storm.

The four gentle cows, never doubting that they would be cared for, munched their hay. In the fitful light of the candle lantern, Anton's massive face looked strangely sober.

"It will be well for one of us to have his supper and then the other, little Franz," he said. "The storm will not grow less, and one of us should be here to reassure the cows if the wind screams too loudly. Do you want to go first?"

"No, you go," Franz urged.

"Very well."

The giant opened the stable door, braced against the wind, slipped into his skis, closed the door and was gone. Franz huddled very close to Caesar while the four cows stamped and munched. He shuddered, not in fear but with awe. This was what winter in St. Bernard Pass truly meant. The wind that sounded inside the stable as a doleful moan, was a screaming demon outside. A strong man would have to struggle just to stand against it.

Twenty minutes later, the stable door opened and Anton came back. He carried a bowl and a dish.

"I have brought your supper, little Franz, for you must remain here," he said. "There is very great trouble. Father Stephen has only now come into the refectory. He is almost spent. A traveler missing from the rest house has not arrived at the Hospice and Father Stephen has been searching for him."

"What now?" Franz asked, with some alarm.

Anton replied, "We all go, little Franz. The Fathers and the maronniers alike, all search for that traveler until he is found. That is our only reason for being here."

"I will eat quickly and be ready at once," Franz said.

Anton smiled gently. "Not you, little Franz. You stay here."

"It was Caesar and I who found Emil Gottschalk!" Franz asserted. "We've searched for lost travelers before!"

"But never in St. Bernard Pass during a storm," Anton reminded him.

"Please—" Franz began.

Anton said shortly, "You stay here."

Anton left and Franz looked dejectedly at the closed stable door. He ate his supper and blew the candle out, for candles must not be wasted. A dozen times during the night he awakened, sure that Anton had returned.

But it was not until past noon of the following day, during a lull in the storm, that Anton did return. From the stable door Franz watched the giant maronnier and two priests of the Hospice. All three were on skis and Anton carried a blanket-wrapped object that had the size and shape of a man. It couldn't possibly be a man, for men were not like that.

Franz watched with staring eyes as the three went to the House of the Dead. When they left it, Anton no longer carried his burden.

11: CAESAR'S SENTENCE

Before the storm spent itself, snow lay twelve feet deep in Grand St. Bernard Pass and some of the drifts were three times as deep. Every cliff and slope held a huge burden of snow, but it was not a burden willingly accepted. And the danger increased a hundred times over.

Enough snow to mold an ordinary snowball might be wind-blown and start more, which in turn gathered more. Finally, carrying boulders, ice and everything else that lay in its path, an all-destroying avalanche would roar down. Such avalanches were a daily occurrence on the peaks about the Hospice.

Franz stood in front of the stable, Caesar beside him. He was watching the sun glance from the surrounding peaks. Wherever it touched snow or ice, it gave back a reflection so dazzling that to face it for more than a few minutes meant to risk blindness. A million jewels, Franz thought, a hundred million jewels, and each one more brilliant than the brightest ornament in any emperor's crown.

The Hospice itself, with ski trails radiating in every direction, like the spokes of a giant wagon wheel, was banked high with snow. Except for the House of the Dead, toward which he looked only when he could not avoid doing so, Franz thought it the most beautiful sight he had ever seen.

Anton Martek, sitting on a chair beside the stable's open door, fashioning a ski pole, did not look up from his work. A complete craftsman, regardless of whether he was honing an ax, making a ski pole, milking a cow, skiing, or doing anything else, Anton believed wholeheartedly that anything worth doing was worth doing well, and it could not be well done unless it received his undivided attention.

Presently, Franz saw a man leave the refectory and ski toward the stable. It was Father Mark, who smiled when he came near and said, "Good afternoon, Franz."

"And a very good afternoon to you, Father Mark," Franz replied. "Have the travelers come up?"

"Not yet," Father Mark told him. "But Fathers Stephen and Benjamin have gone down to guide them. On a day such as this, let us hope there will be no trouble."

"Let us hope so," Franz agreed.

He felt a pang of sorrow. Father Benjamin, who always took Caesar with him when he went down to the rest house, had not even told Franz he was going. But it was not his place, Franz reminded himself, to tell the Fathers what they should or should not do. If Father Benjamin had not asked for Caesar, it was because he did not want him.

Anton Martek stood up respectfully and said, "Good afternoon, Father Mark."

"And to you, Anton." Father Mark noted the half-finished ski pole. "Busy as usual, I see. Well, they do say Satan finds work for idle hands."

Anton said, "I fear he has found enough for mine."

"Tut, tut," Father Mark reproved. "You must not be gloomy on a day so fine. The Prior would speak with you."

"At once," Anton said.

He slipped into his skis and departed with Father Mark. Franz stared wistfully after them. He himself had seen the Prior, in the chapel or from a distance, but he had never dared even think of speaking with him. On those few occasions when their paths would have crossed, and they could not have avoided speaking, Franz had fled as swiftly as possible. Winter in St. Bernard Pass inspired awe, but it was not nearly as awe-inspiring as the Prior of St. Bernard Hospice.

Franz picked up and inspected the ski pole Anton was fashioning, and he tried to fix each detail exactly in his mind. Making proper skis or ski poles was more than just a craft. It was a very precise art, and one that Franz hoped to master some day. Good was not enough. In the Alps, who ventured out on skis took his life in his hands and must have perfection.

A few minutes later, Anton returned alone. He did not look at Franz when he said, "The Prior would talk with you."

"With me?" Franz said bewilderedly. "You," Anton said.

Franz protested, "But—I cannot talk with the Prior!"

"I fear you have no choice, little Franz," Anton told him. "The Prior awaits in the refectory."

Franz asked fearfully, "What does he want, Anton?"

"That you must discover for yourself," Anton replied.

Franz pleaded, "Go with me, Anton!"

"Yes," Anton said quietly, "I will go with you."

Franz put on his skis and, with Caesar trailing, they went to the refectory. The boy's head reeled. His heart fluttered like the wings of a trapped bird. At the entrance to the refectory, he could go no farther.

"Come, little Franz," Anton urged gently.

"Y-yes, Anton." Franz shivered.

Dressed in the habit of his order, the Prior sat before a pile of logs that smoldered in the huge fireplace. With him, and almost as hard to face, were two of the Canons, the Clavandier, whose task it was to watch over Hospice provisions, and two priests.

Franz clasped his hands behind him, so nobody could see them shake, and wished mightily that the floor would open up so he could sink through it.

"It is time we met, young maronnier," the Prior said. "I like to know all who share this work with me. But for some reason, we have never spoken."

"Y-yes, Most Holy Prior," Franz stammered.

"There is nothing to fear," the Prior said.

It was a very gentle voice and, when Franz took courage to look, he saw also that, though it was weather-scarred and storm-beaten, the Prior's was a very gentle face. The boy felt more at ease.

"I am not afraid," he said.

"That is good," the Prior approved. "I wear the Prior's habit and you are a maronnier, but, for all that, we are equal. I have received excellent reports of your diligence and industry. You are a credit to the Hospice."

"Thank you, Most Holy Prior," Franz said.

The Prior smiled, knowing that he should not be addressed in such a fashion but understanding why he was. He continued, "Now that we have finally met, I would that it were for a different reason. I fear that I have sad tidings for you."

"For me?" Franz's heart began to pound again.

"You have a dog," the Prior said, "a great dog that, according to our good Clavandier, eats a great amount of food. Yet, he does no work."

Franz whispered miserably, "That is true."

"Believe me, I understand what this dog means to you." The Prior was very gentle. "I hope to make you understand what the Hospice of St. Bernard means to wayfarers. Every ounce of food we have here is far more precious than gold. Without it, we could neither preserve our own lives nor provide for our guests. It is a harsh order that I must issue, Franz, but with the next travelers who are going there, your dog must be returned to your native village of Dornblatt."

For the moment, Franz was stricken speechless. Then he spoke wildly. "Please!" he begged. "Please do not send Caesar away, Most Holy Prior! It is true that he will not turn the spit, but he saved Father Benjamin from the crevasse! He guided all of us safely to the Hospice while a blizzard raged!"

"That tale I have heard," the Prior said, "and your Caesar surely deserves all praise. But, as you have surely seen for yourself, we have the welfare of travelers well in hand—"

Outside, someone shouted. Those inside looked questioningly toward the door and one of the priests rushed to open it. Looking out, Franz saw two men on skis. One was obviously injured. The other was helping to support him. The unhurt man was Father Benjamin.

The other was Jean Greb, from Franz's native Dornblatt.

12: JEAN'S STORY

Father Mark and Anton rushed to their skis and sped out to help the approaching pair. Father Benjamin surrendered Jean Greb to the mighty Anton, then knelt to undo the harness of Jean's skis. As though Jean, a big man, weighed no more than a baby, Anton Martek cradled him in his arms and carried him into the refectory. He laid him tenderly on a pallet that the Clavandier and one of the Canons had placed in front of the fire.

Franz hung fearfully in the background while the Prior himself, who was skilled in the healing arts, knelt beside the injured man and began to examine him. Jean had fought on while there was need for fighting. Now that the need no longer existed, unconsciousness came.

"I fear that there is no hope for this man's companion," Father Benjamin said in a low voice. "They were coming from the inn to the Hospice when an avalanche rolled down upon them. By a miracle alone, this man was thrown to the top. Not even his skis were broken, and when I discovered him, he was trying to find his companion. I thought it best, even though he protested, to bring him here with all possible speed."

"It was wise to do so," the Prior said quietly. "The snows have claimed many lives. Had you let this man continue to search for his friend, his life might have been lost, too."

"Is Jean badly hurt?" Franz asked huskily.

The Prior glanced up quickly. "Do you know this man, Franz?"

"He is Jean Greb, from my native village of Dornblatt," Franz answered. "He is a very good friend to my family and myself."

"Put your heart at ease." The Prior's slim fingers ceased exploring Jean's body. "There is very great shock, which is not at all extraordinary after one has been the victim of an avalanche. Aside from that, your friend seems to have suffered only a broken arm and some broken ribs. It will be less painful for him if we take the proper measures while he still sleeps."

Anton Martek, who had doubtless discovered Jean's broken arm while carrying him to the Hospice, was suddenly there with splints. Father Mark brought bandages, and all the rest stood silently near while the Prior set and splinted Jean's broken arm and bound his ribs.

Finished, the Prior reached for a flask of brandy that the Clavandier had brought from his stores. He forced a few drops between Jean's lips, waited a moment, then gave the injured man a few more drops.

Jean's eyelids fluttered. He turned his head to one side and moaned. Then he opened his eyes and stared blankly. The Prior knelt before him with a small glass of brandy. He cradled Jean's head with one arm.

"Drink," he said.

Jean sipped slowly, and as he did the color returned to his face and the life to his eyes. He nibbled his own lips. Then the shock faded and he returned to the world of rational beings. His eyes found Franz, and an agony that was born of no physical pain twisted his face.

"We came to see you, Franz," he said in a husky whisper, "and I was the guide. Alas, I was a very poor guide, for the one who engaged me still lies in the snow!"

"It was not your fault," the Prior soothed. "No man can foresee an avalanche."

Franz's heart turned over. For none but the most important of reasons would anyone have set out from Dornblatt to visit him in St. Bernard Pass. Were either of his parents or one of his sisters lost in the snow and not found? Were they beset by some terrible illness? Were—?

"I know there was a message," Jean continued, "but I was not the one who carried it."

"Who was the message from?" Franz burst out.

Jean said, "It was from Emil Gottschalk."

"Emil Gottschalk?" Franz asked bewilderedly.

"The same," Jean said. "It was only two weeks ago that he was able to leave the hospital at Martigny and return to Dornblatt. He has lost one of his feet, but that seems to make small difference, for he has found his heart. His first act was to send for the Widow Geiser and say to her that she may discharge her debt to him at her own will and in her own time. That she will be able to do, since she has such a very fine farm and is shortly to marry Raul Muller. His second act—"

Jean lapsed into silence while Franz's bewilderment grew. Of all the people of Dornblatt who might have sent him a message, Emil Gottschalk was farthest from his thoughts. But the former greedy miser of Dornblatt must surely have come home a changed man. That he had given the Widow Geiser time to pay her debts when he might have foreclosed on her farm was evidence enough of that.

"His second act," Jean went on, "was to compose a message to you. It was a most important message, that must be entrusted only to a most important messenger."

"Who was the messenger?" Franz asked.

Jean answered, "Professor Luttman."

Franz reeled like a bullet-stricken chamois. Professor
Luttman was one of the finest men in Dornblatt. He was a
great and kind teacher, one who had struggled hard to teach
even a stupid Franz Halle. If he and his knowledge were
lost, then all the boys and girls of Dornblatt who might
learn stood a fine chance of growing up to be ignorant
indeed. There would be no one to teach them.

Jean Greb closed his eyes to hide the tears that sprang into
them. He said bitterly, "Would that it were I, and not
Professor Luttman, who lies beneath the snow!"

Franz suddenly forgot that the mountains might tumble if
he spoke to the Prior. He flung himself before the supreme
authority of St. Bernard Hospice.

"Let us go!" he begged. "Let Caesar and me go with
whoever searches for Professor Luttman!"

The Prior said gently, "Your spirit is admirable, Franz, but
this is work for experienced men. You and your dog would
merely hinder them."

"No!" Franz cried. "I can get about on snow! It was Caesar
who found the very Emil Gottschalk whose message
Professor Luttman carries, when experienced men failed!"

"That is true," Jean Greb spoke from his pallet. "Emil
would not be alive today were it not for Franz's dog. He
was buried so deeply in the snow that men alone never
would have found him."

"Your dog can find men buried beneath the snow?" the
Prior questioned.

"Yes!" Franz exclaimed.

The Prior appeared puzzled. "How does he do it?"

"I cannot be sure, but I think he hears the heart beat!" Franz replied. "Let us go! We will hinder no one!"

"I speak for Franz and Caesar," Jean Greb urged. "I have known both all their lives, and I have never known either to hinder anyone. There are few men in Dornblatt who can equal Franz's skill on the snow."

Anton Martek said, "I also speak for Franz. He calls himself stupid because he is unable to understand that which is written in books. But he knows well the arts of the snow and the mountains."

The Prior nodded. "Then go. You too, Anton, and Father Mark. Father Benjamin will guide, and may God go with all of you!"

13: CAESAR'S FEAT

There was a wind, but it was not the roaring blast that so frequently snarled through St. Bernard Pass and it had not tumbled the snow about enough to cover the ski trail left by Father Benjamin and Jean Greb. It was a safe path, for two men had already traveled it in safety. Rather than having to choose carefully a slow and uncertain way, the four could now move swiftly.

Followed only by Caesar, who found the going easy on a path packed by so many skis, Franz stayed just far enough behind Anton Martek to avoid running up on the toboggan the giant pulled. Father Benjamin led the way, followed by Father Mark. There were ropes and shovels on the toboggan.

Franz tried to swallow his heart that insisted on beating in his throat, rather than in his chest. An avalanche was as unpredictable as the chatter of a jay. For all his vast experience in the mountains, Jean Greb had not known this one was coming until it overwhelmed both himself and Professor Luttman. No one could ever be sure.

Franz tried to reassure himself by thinking of the three men ahead of him. All were not only men of the mountains in general, but of St. Bernard Pass in particular. There was no situation that could arise in the Pass which they had not met before and with which they would not know how to cope, Franz told himself. They were very sure of finding Professor Luttman.

But in his own heart, Franz knew how very wrong he could be.

An avalanche was a freakish thing. When tons, and millions of tons, of snow thundered down a slope, it was somewhat comparable to a treacherous river. There were currents that surged toward the top and those that bored toward the bottom. Even though Jean Greb had been cast out on top, Professor Luttman might be lying at the bottom. For all their ability to work miracles, the men of St. Bernard Hospice would never reach him alive if he were. They would never even find him.

Franz tried to banish such gloomy forebodings from his mind and might have succeeded had not one thought persisted. If Father Benjamin believed there was a good chance of finding Professor Luttman, he would have made Jean Greb as comfortable as possible and tried to find him. And in the refectory, while Jean lay unconscious, Father Benjamin himself had said that there was no hope.

Franz thrust a hand behind him and felt a little relieved when Caesar came up to sniff it. He was by no means sure that Caesar could find Professor Luttman, but he was positive that they stood a far better chance with the big mastiff than they ever would without him. He tried to picture in his imagination all the places where the avalanche might have occurred—and gasped with dismay when they finally found it!

The prevailing west wind funneled through a broad gulley. On the east, the gulley was bounded by a gentle slope. But on the west, the slope rose sheer for almost half its height before giving way to an easy rise. The wind had plastered snow against the steep portion. More snow, either wind-borne or falling, had gathered upon it to a depth of twenty feet or more.

It was a much greater burden than the slope should have held. With almost a perpendicular wall, and not a single tree or bush to hold it back, a whisper might set it off and send snow roaring into the gulley. It was a death trap that any experienced mountaineer would recognize at a glance.

Jean Greb, seeing the peril, had chosen to climb above the steep portion on the west slope, rather than veer to the east. It was a choice any mountaineer might have made. But something, possibly the light ski tread of Jean Greb and Professor Luttman, had started the snow on the steep wall rolling. This, in turn, had set off an avalanche on the gentle slope and all of it had poured into the gulley.

In the center of the gulley, snow lay a hundred feet deep. On the north end, where the cleavage between the snow that had rolled and that which had not rolled was almost as sharp as though some colossus had cut it with a knife, there was a near-perpendicular drop that varied between sixty and ninety feet in height. The tremendous force of the avalanche had packed the snow to icy hardness.

Father Benjamin halted, waved his arm and said, "I found your friend here, Franz. He was trying to dig into the snow."

Franz stared with unbelieving eyes at the faint scars in the immense pile of snow. They could have been made only by a ski pole, but a ski pole was the only tool Jean had. Franz knew suddenly that Father Benjamin had been entirely right in bringing Jean to the Hospice. A hundred men with a hundred shovels could not move that mass of snow in a hundred years. It was better to save the man who could be saved than to let him senselessly risk his life for the man who could not.

"You found him here?" Anton Martek asked.

Father Benjamin answered, "This is where the avalanche cast him up. Since he and his companion were traveling very close together, he is sure that his friend cannot be far from this place."

Anton said, "I know of nothing we may do except dig here."

"Nor I," said Father Mark.

Father Benjamin said, "If I had a better idea, I would surely make it known. Let us dig, and let us have faith as we do so."

The boy seized a shovel and began to dig, along with Anton and the two priests. He shook his head in disbelief for, even though he used all his strength, his shovel took only a tiny bite of the hard-packed snow. Despite the cold wind that snapped up the gulley like an angry wolf, beads of perspiration stood out on his forehead....

Franz thought that an hour might have passed when, while the other three continued to dig, he had to stop and rest. For the first time, it occurred to him to look about for Caesar.

The big dog was at the north end of the avalanche, peering over the perpendicular wall. He trotted anxiously back and forth, then leaned over to rest his front paws on a ledge. Suddenly Franz remembered when Caesar had found Emil Gottschalk buried in the snow.

Anton Martek and the two priests remained too busy to notice the boy's departure when he made his way to

Caesar's side. The great mastiff wagged his tail furiously and stared down the wall of snow.

"Is he there?" Franz whispered. "Is he there, Caesar?"

The dog took three paces forward and three back. He whined, leaned over again to rest his front paws on the ledge, then withdrew to his master's side. Franz studied the awful wall that suddenly seemed a thousand feet high, and where a mistake in judgment or a misstep meant possible death and certain injury.

But Caesar would not stop staring down it, and only three feet below was the ledge where he had rested his paws. Franz stepped down, widened the ledge with his shovel and reached behind him to help the dog down. He sought the next ledge that he might dig out with his shovel.

They were halfway down the wall when the boy heard a thunderous, "Franz! Franz! Come back!"

He recognized Father Benjamin's voice but he dared not look back, for even a fairy could not have found more standing room on the thin ledge where the boy and his dog stood. Franz reached down with his shovel to scoop out the next ledge.

After what seemed an eternity, they were at the bottom of the wall.

Caesar ran forward and began to dig in the snow. Scraping beside him, presently Franz found the limp arm of a man.

Cold as the arm was, he could still feel the pulse that beat within it.

14: THE MESSAGE

The fire in the refectory's great fireplace roared. The Prior, the Canons, the Sacristan, and everyone else who lived at the Hospice of St. Bernard and did not have to be away on some urgent business, were gathered around it.

Jean Greb, who felt well enough to sit up by now, occupied a chair in front of the fire. Shaken and thoroughly chilled, but not seriously injured, Professor Luttman lay on Jean's pallet.

The Prior said, "Let us have the dog brought forth. Even though he cannot understand it, he should hear the message."

All eyes turned to Franz, beside whom Caesar had been sitting only recently. The boy looked toward the door.

Caesar, who had accepted the stable but found the refectory much too hot, was waiting just inside the door. His jaws were spread and his tongue lolled. He wagged his tail at Franz and whined, obviously an invitation for his master to open the door and let him out into the comfortable snow.

"He finds the fire much too hot." The boy spoke with a free tongue from a happy heart. He wondered now why he had ever been overawed by the Prior or anyone else at the Hospice. Beneath their somber habits beat very warm and wonderful hearts. If it were any other way, they would not be here. Franz finished, "He wants me to let him out."

"A true dog of the high pass," the Prior said. "Very well, Franz. You may let him out."

The boy walked to the door, opened it, and Caesar trotted out gratefully. He began to roll in the snow. Franz returned to his place.

The Prior said, "All of us know of the miracle, a miracle wrought by a young maronnier and his dog. Now we shall hear the message Professor Luttman carries."

"I have imparted the message to you," Professor Luttman protested. "You are the proper person to tell Franz."

"Not I!" The Prior laughed. "I am merely an onlooker here, and I must say that, for once, I thoroughly enjoy the spectator's role. Proceed, Professor Luttman."

"Very well." The Professor turned to Franz. "Do you know what I really thought the day I expelled you from my school?"

"You thought I was too stupid to learn," Franz replied.

"No such thing!" Professor Luttman denied. "I thought, 'There goes an Alpinist, one who can never discover in my beloved books any of the inspiration that he finds in his beloved mountains. It is truly unjust to keep him in school when he does not belong here.' I thought also that, one day, you would make your mark in the world."

"I am just a maronnier at St. Bernard Hospice," Franz protested.

"And how grateful I am because you are 'just a maronnier,'" Professor Luttman said. "Were you not, I would have died in the snow."

"They would have found you," Franz insisted.

"We would not!" Anton Martek spoke up. "We would have continued digging where we thought he was. It never occurred to any of us that he might be three hundred feet away and down the wall of snow."

"That is true," Father Benjamin agreed.

"Very true," said Father Mark.

"So I am alive today because of you and Caesar," Professor Luttman continued. "Emil Gottschalk lives for the same reason. He wanted to give you—" Professor Luttman named a greater sum of money than the boy had ever thought existed.

"I would not accept his money," Franz asserted firmly.

Professor Luttman said, "So I told him, so your father told him, too, but both of us agreed that the Hospice of St. Bernard might well use it. Now the Prior and I have talked, and the Prior declares that you shall decide how that money may be spent."

Franz murmured, "I would like enough to keep Caesar in food, so that he will not be sent away from the Hospice."

The Prior laughed. "If there was any danger of Caesar being sent away—and there isn't the slightest—there is enough money to feed him for the next hundred years and a vast sum besides."

Franz looked appealingly at the Prior. "I am not worthy to spend a sum so huge!"

"You must," the Prior told him. "No one else can."

Franz turned his troubled eyes to the floor. After a moment, he looked up.

"There is only one thing I would do," he said finally. "I would go down into the villages, the mountain villages where people and animals alike must learn the arts of the snow. I would buy more Alpine Mastiffs, dogs such as Caesar, and bring them to the Hospice. I am sure you may find someone with sufficient skill to train them properly."

"And I am equally sure we already have someone," the Prior declared. "His name is Franz Halle. This is a day of great joy for all of us. Think of the lives that would have been lost but will be saved after we have these—

"These dogs of St. Bernard."

JIM KJELGAARD

was born in New York City. Happily enough, he was still in the pre-school age when his father decided to move the family to the Pennsylvania mountains. There young Jim grew up among some of the best hunting and fishing in the United States. He says: "If I had pursued my scholastic duties as diligently as I did deer, trout, grouse, squirrels, etc., I might have had better report cards!"

Jim Kjelgaard has worked at various jobs—trapper, teamster, guide, surveyor, factory worker and laborer. When he was in his late twenties he decided to become a full-time writer. No sooner decided than done! He has published several hundred short stories and articles and quite a few books for young people and adults.

His hobbies are hunting, fishing, dogs and questing for new stories. He tells us: "Story hunts have led me from the Atlantic to the Pacific and from the Arctic Circle to Mexico City. Stories, like gold, are where you find them. You may discover one three thousand miles from home or, as in The Spell of the White Sturgeon, (winner of the Boys' Life— Dodd, Mead Prize Competition) right on your own door step." And he adds: "I am married to a very beautiful girl and have a teen-age daughter. Both of them order me around in a shameful fashion, but I can still boss the dog! We live in Phoenix, Arizona."

Manufactured by Amazon.ca
Bolton, ON